E.R.E.

ELECTRIC RINGWORLD EARTH

ERIC WILKINS

Published by:

OMNIBOOK CO.
99 Wall Street, Suite 118
New York, NY 10005
USA
+1-866-216-9965
www.omnibookcompany.com

For e-book purchase: Kindle on Amazon, Barnes and Noble
Book purchase: Amazon.com, Barnes & Noble, and
www.omnibookcompany.com

Omnibook titles may be purchased in bulk for educational, business,
fund-raising, or sales promotional use. For more information please
e-mail info@omnibookcompany.com

CONTENTS

CHAPTER 1
CONNECTING EARTH'S POLES

As Humanity approached the dawn of the twenty second century, it was inevitable that a new way of thinking prevailed upon citizens of planet Earth that occurred around the year 2200.

In order to explain the futures existence, one must first explain how it all began and the exact details of what first occurred way back in the late 21st and early part of the 22nd century.

It was in the year 2205 that time travel was first achieved and introduced into humanities future endeavor.

In that year, there existed deep underground a space time research laboratory named Future Technologies.

Experiments there had continued for over two decades on exactly how to accomplish safe non intrusive time travel.

It was well known that Planet Earth was indeed a super dynamo itself. In order to acquire the extreme power needed to accomplish time travel, a secrete black project had been started back in the year 2195. That secrete project was entitled Talaxia.

Talaxia was disguised as an underground fuel pipeline system that was created to resolve the planets petrol fuel shortage and delivery system. Since crude oil was discovered beneath both of Earth's north and south poles, Talaxia was the perfect disguise for Future Technologies attempt to tap into the extreme electric power that would be produced if a three meter diameter electric conductor wire from both poles, were joined together at Earth's equator.

Each three meter diameter wire was inserted a kilometer deep at each pole of the Earth and joined together at step down transformer stations near Future Technologies laboratory.

The step down transformers existed near our research station that existed underground also at the equator.

Connecting the current of opposite poles of Planet Earth together at the equator, would indeed tap into Earth's extreme dynamo effect.

Head of research at Future Technologies was Professor Briana Paldagus.

Briana, was now a 31 year old female professor that graduated from Cornell University in the year 2195. She was now in charge of the secrete Talaxia project that was soon to be connected near the transformer station on the equator of Earth.

It was inevitable for the Talaxia Project to be kept secrete because no one knew how much electricity or exactly what would happen once the north and south poles three meter diameter cables were connected and engaged.

Two giant step down transformers were built at the equator in attempts to control the power flow on a percentage basis.

In the present year of 2215 it was Professor Briana Paldagus that was in charge of the secrete Talaxia Project in order to supply enough power to the time travel project that was invented by myself and conducted by me Professor Irric Wapello.

Myself Professor Wapello, had created an ingenious time machine that required at least a million terra watts of power to initiate transmission of one human being into the past or future.

It was assumed that the Earth's polar connections would produce at least a thousand times that amount of electricity. But assuming is a dangerous precedent to engage.

In actuality, No one knew exactly how much power would be created or exactly what tapping into this tremendous power source would actually do. But, in this present year of 2215 it was indeed a risk that myself and other scientist were willing to take.

There were extreme hopes that if all went well, for the first time in history, a human would soon be able to at least glimpse into humanities past and future.

CHAPTER 2

FIRST TIME MACHINE TEST

On that daring Monday morning of July the eighth 2215, the first stage test of the polar connection was to be tested for the actual amount of current that would be produced.

Professor Paldagus stood at the controls and gave the order to bring both step down transformers online.

At 8:16 AM that Monday morning, she gave the order to introduce electric current at .05 percent to the power grid. The switch board lit up immediately measuring five thousand Terra Watts of power into the power grid.

The control room was buzzing with fascination as the power meter registered five thousand Terra Watts at only a half of a percent power test.

Professor Wapello's face was beaming with smiles as he realized that the extreme power that he had always needed to energize his time machine had finally been accomplished.

Many more test were ran the following Tuesday morning at one percent power the electric energy registered well over ten thousand Terra Watts.

CHAPTER 3
TALAXIA'S CONSTRUCTION

I will now go back 15 years to explain the details of the Talaxia's Construction

The extreme Talaxia wiring system was laid out and installed over the past 15 years and the total length of the wiring accomplished was just over 12,500 miles or just over 20,116 kilometers long that joined together at the equator from both poles of the Earth.

That total length equaled to six billion, six hundred million feet of three meter thick conduction tube wire that was installed.

Each connected section of pipeline cable was a hundred feet long so that made a total of 660,000 sections of one hundred feet long connecting cables that had to been joined together and buried ten feet underground to accomplish the super equator power station connection.

Such a black project was very expensive but in order to accomplish the power that was required to power Professor Wapello's goal of accomplishing time travel, it was an expense that was considered well spent.

There were struggling times early on in 2196 when the polar cables were being drilled deep into the Artic of both the north and south poles that was very hard to accomplish.

At the very tips of each Earth rotation point, huge crews of artic construction workers struggled daily to work drilling crews in the frigid polar temperatures.

In order to drill through the thick ice to a depth of a kilometer deep into the frozen poles, that process alone took well over three years time just to accomplish a deep four meter diameter hole at each pole.

One can imagine that the process at the Antarctic took a bit longer due to the extreme temperature difference at the south pole. That was all irrelevant now because the pole wire insertions had been completed by the year 2200.

It took a grand total of 15 years for the land laying wire crews to complete the 12,500 miles of underground and under sea wire installation to be connected to the equatorial power base station.

Each wiring burial crew averaged a little over a tenth of a mile a day in their 15 year long attempt to connect the huge electric wires.

So on average, each crew from both polar wire layers, were installing approximately 18, one hundred feet long sections a day to accomplish the entire length of 12,500 miles of three meter thick wired pipeline connection.

That's pretty remarkable considering the entire length of the Earth from poles to the equator. So in actuality, that brings us up to date in the year 2215 when the wired line was first completed and the first actual power test were being conducted.

July 16th 2215, The first power stages had been completed and up to 5 percent power had been tested at a remarkable power supply of 500,000 Terra Watts obtained so far at 10 percent power test. Extreme power indeed.

Though the power supply was much more capable at a higher percentage rate, it was estimated at the rate of percentage change that power equal to at least fifty percent or 15,000,000 Terra Watts would be required to operate the time machine.

CHAPTER 4

MICKEY'S JOURNEY TEST

July 20th 2215, We at the Facility celebrated this date in 1969 when humankind first set foot upon the Moon. To all of us it was a more exciting Saturday morning because everything had been made ready to test the first animal object test of Professor Wapello's time machine.

This first attempt would be to send a small white mouse though to the future and after 60 seconds of time had elapsed, to immediately return the tiny creature to the laboratory for examination.

We named the little white test mouse Mickey. Mickey was securely incased in a one foot square cage to insure that it wouldn't escape during the one minute test to the future and back.

If all went well with this test, the next step would be to send a larger animal in two days on Monday July 22nd, 2215.

Briana and I Irric, stood that morning in front of the room sized time apparatus with Mickey and cage sitting atop a pedestal perched five feet above the floor. A lab technician reached inside the cage and finished attaching a tiny recorder camera around the brave little mouse's neck.

I had decided to send Mickey ahead in time to exactly one year in the future to the exact spot that he occupied on the laboratory pedestal. We were certainly sure that this spot in the future would still exist and considered that to be a safe first step test.

9:05 Am EST, Briana brought the power up to 150,000 terra watts and I engage the time machine as we both watched Mickey and the cage disappear and fade into nothingness.

The 60 second return timer clicked away and as the clock counted down from sixty seconds, the timer approached zero while Mickey and cage reappeared exactly upon the pedestal where it had departed from a minute ago. It appeared only as Mickey and cage had been invisible for a minute and then suddenly reappeared.

Little Mickey appeared normal as he twitched his tiny nose as if nothing unusual had even occurred. Let's see what the video camera reveals Briana spoke up.

A staff technician named Anna Parson that had installed the tiny camera was now reaching into the cage to remove it and proceeded across the laboratory to plug the device into the control board to view the contents of the 60 second recording.

A video appeared upon the screen displaying the laboratory with a room full of technicians and Briana and myself moving around being visible in the video.

The sound revealed us talking about the potential possibility of sending two people ahead in time together as the clip abruptly ended after a minute had elapsed.

We two professors looked at each other with big smiles and considered this first test a complete success.

All of a sudden to our surprise, Mickey and cage began glowing and lit up with a bright flash and instantly disappeared again.

We both were immediately stunned at what had just occurred. What the heck happened Briana asked. I'm not Sure I responded. It's obvious that Mickey went through to the future by the recording results but where the mouse disappeared to is beyond my comprehension.

Okay Briana replied, we'll definitely have to do a lot of research on the error before we can try again.

The next thirty days consisted of extreme research on the possible error that had happened to little Mickey.

It was finally realized that not enough power had been stored in the tiny return capacitor that was attached to Mickey's body.

The capacitors stored charge was just not enough stored power to enable a stable return of the tiny mouse.

CHAPTER 5
MINNIE'S JOURNEY TEST

Monday August 19th, 2215, four weeks later at 10:15 AM,

Another attempt was being made with a female mouse specimen named Minnie.

This time the tiny return storage capacitor had been doubled in storage capability in hopes that Minnie mouse would return safely and stabilize.

Instead of a fifteen percent power charge, the total power was increased to twenty percent of the Talaxia output. This one minute one year trip into the future produced a stable return of Minnie exactly to the podium cage she occupied.

The tiny camera was quickly removed from Minnie and we in the lab stood by with bated breath waiting to see if Minnie would stay stabilized.

An hour passed and little Minnie seemed to show no ill affects from the journey forward one year in time.

The video recording showed nothing unusual except the furniture was in a different orientation and no humans were present in the laboratory in the middle of the night.

Now with this success the experiments could move ahead with a chimpanzee specimen on the next attempt.

CHAPTER 6
BONZO'S TIME TEST

Wednesday August 21st, A male chimpanzee named Bonzo sat perched in a locked cage atop of the transfer podium with all of the recording apparatus attached and ready to be sent into the future.

This time, the forward future time was set to project Bonzo ahead two years into the year 2228. Bonzo was to stay in the future in his cage for a total of ten Minutes before his capacitor would energize his return to the Lab.

Since Bonzo's transport, the timer had continuously counted down from 600 seconds until the count reached the time of return. Upon the approached of zero, Bonzo suddenly reappeared in a wavy watery-like return to the perched podium in front of all present.

Lab assistants quickly recovered the camera attached to Bonzo and immediately engaged it into the computer's projection view.

Obvious at first, was that the sound on the video was distorted but the video itself was mostly intact.

There was a scene that showed Myself and Briana looking extremely happy and the entire staff was celebrating some sort of success but, the sound was extremely distorted and it was not obvious as to what exactly we were celebrating two years into the future.

The sound was available but it took the lab assistants several weeks to fine tune the video to export the details of what was said in the future. The sound revealed that the entire staff were celebrating Anna Parson's

33rd birthday. There was nothing unusual revealed in the sound track so the Bonzo test resumed.

Experiments were progressing steadily ahead for the next few month as I, Professor Irric Wapello continued to fine tune the process of getting the time machine calibrated to handle more power input.

Bonzo's test continued to be the lab experiment and up to this point in time, he had been reenergized back several times. Bonzo had been projected further into the future until Professor Briana and I had decided that it was now safe to attempt the first human into the future's unknown existence.

Myself Professor Irric, had decided to be the first human being to be projected into the future.

This time, the time machine was set for me to be sent ahead into the year 3,000. My first attempt would allow me to only stay in the future for a period of 24 hours and it was my intention to record the results before returning to the present.

Head time machine technician Norius Armstrong was now in control at the inducer control to engage the process of sending me through to the year 3000.

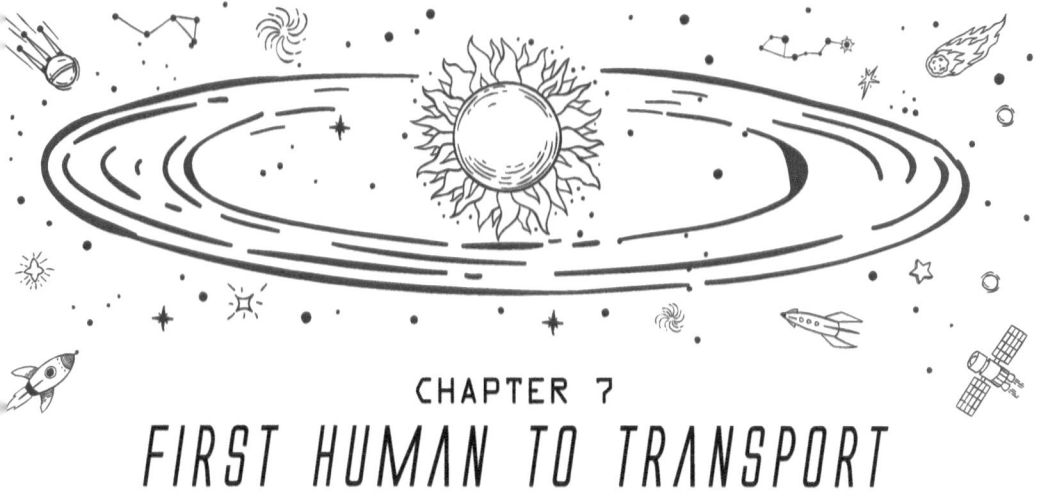

CHAPTER 7
FIRST HUMAN TO TRANSPORT

It was 2 PM, November 23rd, 2226 as I Professor Irric sat perched upon the transport ready to be the first human being sent ahead into the future. Yes I was a bit scared but excitement and curiosity overcame my fear. I thought back in history of Armstrong's first step on the Moon. Astronauts of that day were indeed brave souls. I had to be brave now when it counts for myself.

Norius brought the Talaxia power source up to fifty one percent capacity and the transducers hummed and buzzed intensely as the thumbs up signal was given from me to proceed with the transport.

In the beginning there were lightning's crackle snaps of power as Norius Armstrong engaged the sequence to transport me.

I watched the room disappear and it felt as if I were falling head over heals forward through a spinning tunnel with a distant glowing vision of earth in the far away tunnel's end.

It seemed as if minutes passed while swirling inside a wormed shaped tunnel but in a sudden light speed instant, I rolled forward to a cool dark lab floor. I was a bit dazed but conscious of the new surroundings that I had just arrived.

The underground laboratory was now dark dusty and deserted. Cobwebs filled the corners and water dripped from overhead and seeped down along murky walls that once was the underground base that I once knew.

I had no idea of what happened to the base and if I was even in the year 3000. I struggled in the darkness to find a small penlight key chain that I always carried in my right front pocket.

As I engaged the small flashlight, I was startled suddenly by a flock of bats that burst into flight near the ceiling in a sudden screech of flight over my head.

Touching my way through the darkness, I managed to find my way to where the now defunct elevator and its stairwell to the left existed.

Slowly I pried the creaky stairwell door open revealing the extremely cobwebbed steps that led upward towards a high above light source.

My nervous left hand was clinging to rusted stair rail as I continuously brushed the spider webs away with a broom in my right hand that I had retrieved from a dark corner along the way.

I began climbing higher and higher towards the upper level light source continuously swishing webs with the broom in front of me as I climbed the reversing stairwell higher toward the brilliant light above.

I had not realized before just how deep the base was below ground because the elevator always had been my entrance to the underground base.

I climbed on higher becoming a bit exhausted as I neared the finale reverse flight of stairs and stepped out onto the sunlit level's exit.

The air smelled like burnt tinfoil. The air was 95 degree Fahrenheit hot but still breathable.

The Brilliant sunlight caused temporary blindness for a minute or so until my eyes became adjusted to the bright sunshine that I now encountered.

CHAPTER 8

MY FIRST SIGHT
OF THE RINGWORLD

Blurry at first was a sight that I had trouble distinguishing. There was an entire bright half circle reflection high overhead I couldn't believe what I was now focusing on.

As far as I could see past the curvature of the horizon, were many giant columns reaching skyward all the way above the clouds to the edge of space and attached to a tubular ring system in space above Earth..

Planet Earth now had rings connected by many round kilometer diameter thick sky reaching connecting ring columns.

It was amazing!. Earths equator region east and westbound had continuous giant columns that were attached to a tubular ring system high over my head. How could this be I questioned.

How could technology have changed so much in 774 years I wondered. Many early thoughts were running through my mind by the many questions that I was pondering.

I knew that in my time that the Laboratory was located far away from a city but even in the distance back then, you could see evidence of a city on the far northern horizon. That cities light source was not discernible anymore.

The most amazing reality was that there were no humans in sight on the surface anywhere at this moment in time.

I stood above the former labs underground stairwell entrance. I took a giant breath of this future earth air and it was very hot but seemed perfectly palatable with oxygen.

What had happened I wondered. Did all humans now live in the giant Ringworld that I was seeing directly overhead?

I could not see one single human being anywhere on the Earth's surface.

I looked left and right long and hard and decided that the closest column from my position was in the easterly direction and I estimated it to be five kilometers away.

It appeared to be high noon and I began walking towards the east. I stayed out of the bright sunlight and walked in the shade that was cast upon the Earth by the ring's shadow upon the surface.

At a fast walking pace of about eight kilometers per. hour, it took me about 38 minutes to reach the backside of the base of the closest sky reaching column structure.

It was huge and about 1.9 kilometers around in it's circumference.

It's color was a cool white that tapered off out of site past clouds and it had the texture of smooth ceramic upon my touch.

It seemed as if I had arrived at the structure and no door or entrance was in sight anywhere on the upward sky bounding structure.

As I continued my journey around the right edge of the ceramic roundness of the giant column, it took another 20 minutes to follow a quarter of the structures circumference and finally arrived at a peculiar looking entrance on the South side of the column.

Deeply engraved with 12 inch blood red numbers was the number 21. The number was above a circular five meter diameter blue door.

There were no seams or windows or anything else to be described upon the structure except that to the right side, there was a 3 by 3 inch touch pad displaying numbers 1 through 10.

Still no humans in sight I tried my luck at guessing the possible code. My favorite number was 3.14 so I nervously punched in that specific code.

CHAPTER 9
THE DOOR OPENS

Suddenly, a booming voice warning occurred asking me to state my business and the door silently rolled open sideways to the left and two armed guards stood inside pointing mysterious looking weapons towards my head.

Who are you bellowed the six foot tall male guard. His uniform was like no military uniform I'd ever seen. Answer the question the second guard spoke even louder. I was startled but answered nervously. I am Irric Wapello and I appear to be lost at the moment I replied. Lost from where the first guard responded. You know the law. No one is allowed to walk the surface while the sun is overhead. It's the law he shouted.

Little did I know at the time that the Sun's energy had increased over the past five centuries and had I not stayed in the shadow of the ring system, I would have been burned by the Sun's bright radiation. I did learn later that the ozone no longer existed.

Get out of the sunlight the second guard shouted. Step inside now before we close the door and leave your lost soul to fry in the radiation.

I did so instantly and for the first time observed the beginning inner structure of pylon number 21.

My time to remain here was 22 hours and 28 minutes before my charged capacitor would instantly reenergize me back to the year that I was from.

I tried to conceal my backpack but the lead guard grabbed me and removed it from my shoulder harness. I need that I protested loudly but he didn't seem to care about my objection. The guard held the gray backpack above his head to examine it from the bottom then sat it to the floor beside the door I had just entered and now had closed behind me..

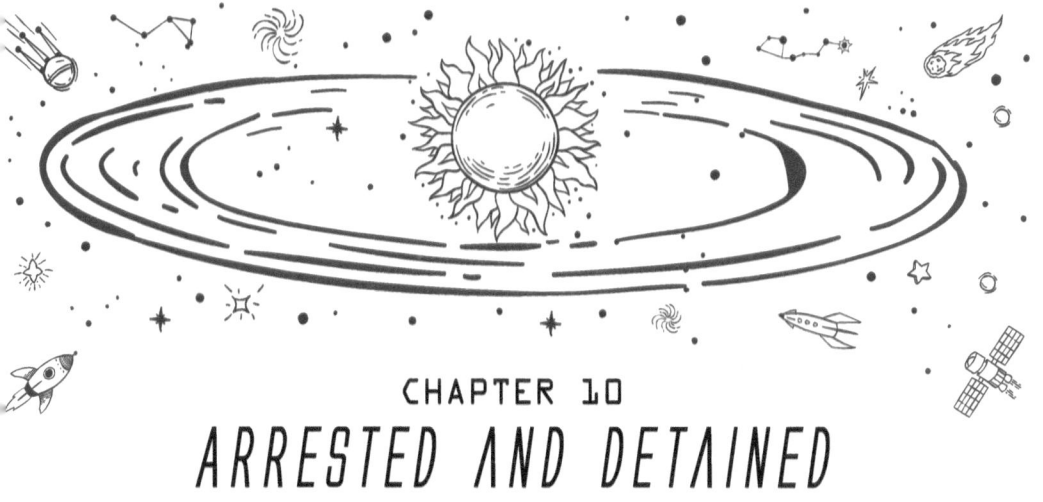

CHAPTER 10
ARRESTED AND DETAINED

You're under arrest one guard shouted as he cuffed my hands behind me and forcefully ushered me further inward towards a second green five meter round door. I looked back and noticed that the second guard now carried the backpack that I needed to return home while the first guard demanded me forward.

The second door opened silently and the entire inside was displayed to my view as we walked towards a far station along the left inner wall.

There were at least a 500 masked humans working at a task around pits of bubbling goo.

I couldn't quite comprehend at the moment exactly what they were accomplishing but the air was stale with ceramic dust and 100 foot strands of steel rebar were stacked in stored holder racks for retrieval.

I was quickly led to a smaller door that slid open to reveal a staunch uniformed officer sitting behind a 3D projected desk.

This human was on the outside in the daylight the guard explained to the officer in charge.

He had this backpack apparatus that he hasn't explained yet. He says that his name is Irric Wapello.

The head officer in charge looked up from his 3D computer screen to observe this peculiar dressed human that stood between guards before him.

I'm head security Officer Dalon Riggan and I demand to know what you were doing outside during daylight hours. We here at Pylon 21 have strict rules about humans being exposed to the deadly sunlight. Exactly who are you and where did you come here from, he questioned intensely.

My mind was racing with deceptive thoughts as I pondered how to reply to the officers strict questioning.

I finally received the courage to reply. Sir, all I know is that I awoke in a abandoned underground bunker several kilometers away and my memory before that point in time is uncertain. I don't recall how I got there I said. It's a mystery to me.

I was trying to conceal my lies but the head officer seemed to sense that I wasn't telling the truth.

How can a human not know where they come from he bellowed out loud towards me. Are you a spy he asked with an indignant burst of anger. You're lying he stated.

I noticed again that the second guard had retrieved my backpack and had dropped it in the corner as we entered the officers quarters.

Sir I responded, please believe me, I'm not sure where I came here from but I do know that I need that backpack to return home.

That statement seemed to make the officer even madder.

Take him to lockup and hand that backpack over to the head scientist and have it analyzed he ordered. You should have never brought that thing near me before you had it analyzed he shouted at the two guards. Get him and that backpack out of here now he ordered.

One guard grabbed my clutched strapped wrist and ushered me towards the exit. We walked at least a quarter of a kilometer through the pylon and came to a room that I was pushed into and a force field was applied to the door's exit.

I watched intently through the opening as one of the guards walked over to a female person not too far away and handed the backpack to the masked woman sitting at another 3D desk.

From this distance I couldn't hear their words but I did notice the guard was telling her something while motioning back towards where I was then towards the head officers office door.

I'd arrived here in the year 3000 about four hours ago and I knew that in 20 hours from now that if I didn't have that backpack on that I would never be able to return to my century.

I also knew that if I had explained to the officer that I was a time traveler from the past he would never have believed my explanation of how I got here.

Before this is over, I may have to reveal my circumstance to the officer but here at the moment, I chose to delay that fact and remain somewhat anonymous.

Two more hours passed since I was locked up and four hours since I had arrived in the future. Eventually, another guard came and disengaged the force field and led me to an elevator that I assumed would carry me to the Ringworld above.

He spoke not a word as the elevator door slid silently open and he motioned for me to step in ahead of himself.

He was armed with the strangest weapon I'd ever seen and the thing appeared to resemble a three inch horseshoe or more like a u shaped two pronged golden magnet. The guard kept it on his right hip and I was still cuffed hands behind me with a plastic tie strip.

The up shaft elevator began moving softly at first and sped up quickly as I could now feel extra G force as the upward device sped up.

Still in silence the guard spoke not a word as approximately 20 minutes passed and I sensed the elevators speed begin to start decreasing.

Another several minutes passed and suddenly the floor pivoted 180 degrees upside down and the elevator stopped and the door opened.

I immediately noticed that gravity was present but it seemed slightly stronger than gravity was when I was at ground level.

I estimated it to be about ten percent stronger than it was before we stepped into the elevator.

We stepped from the elevator to the upside down floors that was now oriented in the same direction that the elevator had pivoted to.

I found myself totally fascinated as I began looking down at the many tube spokes with a glass-like view of the beautiful planet below.

I estimated the diameter of the round ring to be three hundred meters or at least a thousand feet.

I was immediately escorted by the same guard to the center of the tube where a double east west two way tubular transport system was located.

Humans entered and exited the inner ring transport system traveling to their specific pylon predetermined destinations.

We stepped into the transport car outside the tube and once loaded the tube car slid inward and began moving swiftly inside the tubes.

There were two separate parallel tubes depending on which direction you wanted to travel.

The guard and I sat down and fastened a seatbelt in padded chairs with our backs to the east in the west bound tube car as it methodically entered the clear tube transport and began moving rapidly passing many floor sections in the process. Their were open view sections between the pylons that revealed land and oceans and clouds as we fell westward.

I could sense almost zero gravity as we fell westward against rotation through the inner ring transport system.

I could read the digital control panel on the front of the transport. It displayed that the entire circumference of the Ringworld above and around Earth was approximately 79,445 miles in total length.

The entire Ringworld system was supported from the ground up by 36 individual columns like the number 21 column I was brought up in.

I had also figured out that there were 360 different long sections in the ring system relating to the 360 degrees in a circle and by now I had figured out that the ring system was 200 miles above the surface and was a total of 79,445 miles or 127,854 kilometers total distance around and above the Earth.

The westbound transport was now moving at about 700 miles per hour and after a twenty minute ride it began slowing and in several more minutes slowed to a stop at a level numbered 175.

It seemed so strange to me that this transport guard had not spoken a word this entire time. I was scared but determined to keep my wits about my situation. I was in their world of which I knew very little about up until this point. I simply didn't know what to expect or where the guard was taking me. I thought about speaking to him but I knew the less I said the better off I was.

The transport we occupied came to a stop, then rotated ninety degrees on our backs and exited the system and slid out onto a raised platform with steps leading down to the outside ring floor.

The canopy opened up without a sound and he motioned for me to step to the platform below the doors exit.

I finally spoke to the guard and asked him where he was taking me and he shook his head no and patted his weapon on his right holstered hip. I began to be a bit more concerned at that point.

We went down the stairs and walked towards a lit office door almost two hundred meters away. As we got closer I could see the numbers 175 lit up above the office door.

CHAPTER 11
THE OMNIPOTENT PAZ

The guard reached ahead and inserted a pass code number and the door swished open to surprising details to behold.

I had always considered the possibility of aliens but at this moment I was indeed very surprised at the creature that occupied inside the room that the guard had escorted me into.

There before me was a creature that was hard to describe in human language. It whistle popped a sound as it moved and never occupied the same space in any given second. It continuously flashed different colors at any spot that it presently was at in the room.

As the guard departed the room the door closed behind him and I realized that I was alone with this what ever it was and became extremely scared at my present circumstance.

I could best describe it visually as a fast moving color changing black light human sized flashing hummingbird. The visual of it continuously moved around very fast making it hard to discern or even describe in words.

Instantly without out words or sounds that the alien being exchanged, I could senses that my thoughts and mind were being probed without my consent. I tried hard to block the connection but the creatures power was just too powerful to resist its unstoppable mind probe.

There was a tingling fuzzy feeling in my brain that was almost to the extent of pain and the harder I tried resisting the more painful it became. Then as quickly as it had begun it finally ceased.

The entire time the creature continuously disappeared and reappeared in a different parts of the enclosed room.

Words came into my head as it finally communicated in English with a feminine child like voice.

You're human but not from this century it said. From the year 2126 you have come in your first human attempt at your time travel experiment.

I am designated as Paz by humans and you have been sent to me to ascertain the truth of your existence. No lies can pass my mind without the truth being revealed.

I will refer to you as Irric of past from this moment in time forward. You are now allowed a reasonable inquiry.

Nervously I spoke out loud but it quickly issued an objection and stopped my words from being sounded out loud.

Human voices are hurtful to my being it spoke to my mind. You only need to think your thoughts and I will hear.

A thousand thoughts were going through my mind and the creature responded before I could stop thinking.

I hear all that is in your thoughts it replied before I could finish thinking up many questions. I didn't have to say a word before the Paz began replying to my thoughts.

My real designation is way to complicated for humans to pronounce in your feeble minds it said.

My kind is from a planet humans refer to as Gliese 581 C. My planet is 20 light years or 120 trillion miles from your Sun in the constellation Libra.

Our planet that we refer to as Dimonda orbits our star very close at 6.2 million of your Earth miles. Dimonda is tidally locked to our star and my kind exist in the shadows of the backside.

The Paz received a message from humans that originated from Earth in the year 2008 and received in 2029 at Gliese 581 C. In the year 2230 we ventured here to your world and made first contact with the humans of this world.

After a short war that we immediately won, We then became rulers over humankind and taught them some of our physics and how to build this Ringworld around planet Earth.

The short war destroyed the ozone in Earth's atmosphere and the remainder of humankind was forced to exist here under our control after the war was over.

The Ringworld construction began in the year 2332 and was completed by my race and humans in Earth year 2399.

I and my kind are to be referred to only as Paz. That is a command that I expect to be followed.

Your pathetic attempt of time travel is to be stopped and no communication will be allowed to occur between your past human beings.

You Irric of past, shall be returned to quarantine and held in stasis until I make a decision on your status.

Your return to your time will be stopped and the return mechanism will be destroyed.

You will remain in this century under our control until I make a decision on what can be done about your future existence.

Suddenly again the door behind me opened and there stood the same no words guard that had escorted me here.

The guard stood motionless for a few seconds and then stepped inside and ushered me towards the door. As I exited Paz told me that he was the only one of his race here aboard the Ringworld. The remainder of his kind were in ships orbiting the Ringworld system around Earth.

He informed me that his mind was so powerful that he was able to control all humans aboard the Ringworld system.

I had wondered why the guard hadn't spoken. Evidently all the humans above and below the Ringworld were controlled by the great Paz that I had been just introduced to.

Except for the guards at lower 21 column, no humans had spoken to me. Evidently, all of humankind was now under the control of the Paz and his kind.

I was escorted still in plastic cuffs back to upper column section above column 21 on the east bound transport.

The words of Paz just kept running through my mind the entire journey back. Even now I could feel his mind probing my thoughts even a great distance from his presence.

Somehow I had to escape this madness but I kept preventing my mind to even think about it for the moment because I knew that even this far away that the Paz could sense my thoughts.

The guard escorted me back to the section we had came from and to the column 21 down elevator and upon arrival I was being escorted towards the original holding cell that I had first occupied at the lower base of column 21.

CHAPTER 12
MY ESCAPE 3000

I knew the great Paz could read my thoughts even at a great distance but my solution to blocking his mind control was to keep repeating this long ago ditty in my head of a musical tune from my childhood days on earth.

The ditty went like - Let me see said the blind man, as he picked up the hammer and saw.

Over and over I kept intensely repeating that same riddle phrase as I was being returned back towards the holding cell that I was first put in at the lower column 21 station at Earth's ground level.

Let me see said the blind man, as he picked up his hammer and saw!

I knew that my time here was getting shorter because I still had my digital time chip attached inside my left wrist that informed to me a continuous countdown.

I had less than one hour to somehow escape this extreme situation and retrieve my backpack and return to my own century.

As the elevator reached the ground level, I just kept repeating that riddle ditty in my head over and over to block my thoughts from being comprehended by the Paz.

The downovator door slid open and I was being escorted and still handcuffed behind my back with a plastic tie. Across the Round floor towards my original holding cell in the middle I could see my backpack now sitting on the female scientist desk that was in charge of examining it.

I was escorted within a hundred feet of where my backpack was placed.

It just so happened at that very moment that a large crated ceramic requirement object was being brought in from the outside and I noticed that the door was in the process of slowly beginning to close. There was an absent moment of sound.

Without any pre thought, I suddenly broke free of the escort guard and stepped aside and grabbed the backpack from the table with my cuffed hands and ran as fast as I could towards the closing door to the outside.

Just as I approach the circular closing exit, a laser blast just missed my leg as I was barely able to slip through the remaining closing of the door towards the second door that was still open to the outside world just as the first door finished closing.

I ran outside to my right as hard and as fast as I could while holding on to my backpack still clutched behind me in my trembling hands.

I ran hard around the outside of the curved huge column. If I could just make it back to the deserted underground bunker that I had arrived here in, I knew I would be safe.

I kept twitching and turning my head as I ran with all my might trying to see if any guards were chasing me.

Due to the curvature of the kilometer diameter round column I could see no one chasing me but I just knew that they couldn't be far behind.

I also knew that in order to get back to my own century that I had to return to my former underground bunker.

I'd have to run 5 more kilometers without being captured.

My hands were still cuffed and I kept looking as I ran to find something to cut the plastic tie so that I could manage to put the backpack on and change my center of gravity while running.

CHAPTER 13
ESCAPE TO THE BUNKER

There was nothing but brown burnt grass between the backside of column 21 and the direction that I had came here from. I didn't have a choice. I had to run out into the sunlight.

Hampered by the backpack that I was carrying with my cuffed hands, I made the decision to take off running in the direction towards the deserted bunker.

The weight of the backpack was only 15 pounds but I couldn't run as fast as I would have been able to if my hands had been free.

I remember falling once to the ground and getting up as fast as I could while looking back to see if I was being followed by the guards or possibly the Paz aliens.

Far back just coming into view around column 21, I could see a mile or so behind me in the distance two human figures that began moving towards me.

I got up and began running again as fast as I possibly could still carrying the backpack.

Suddenly in my path I discovered a long deserted broken glass bottle that I immediately picked up by the neck and smashed it against a nearby rock.

It took me about 30 seconds to manage to cut the cuff tie and I then hurriedly slung the backpack over my arms and shoulder and without looking back I started running faster than before with my center of gravity more stable and the ability to pump my arms as I ran.

Every now and then I'd look back and noticed that the two guards were still running after me and were about a mile or so behind me.

I ran even faster after that.

I could see about two kilometers away in the distance the area where the underground bunker was that I arrived here from.

I was no longer in the shade of the Ringworld above and I could feel my exposed skin beginning to tingle. I was being burned by the sun's rays. It was 11:48 AM and the suns rays were intense as I approached the stairwell downwards.

I managed to look back again and I could no longer see the guards chasing me. I surmised that maybe they too were being burned by the sun's rays also. I hopefully prayed that they had turned around and headed back to the safety of column 21.

I had to hurry up and get down to the lower bunker transport position. 180 Seconds remained on my timer.

Even in the darkness, I could feel the effects of the sunburn that had been eating away of my exposed flesh.

Totally out of breath I breeched the ten levels of winding stairwell downward to the laboratory. I fell exhausted to the cold floor.

CHAPTER 14

REENERGIZED HOME TO 2226

My return to my centuries timer still had ninety three seconds before it would energize me back to the year 2226 and the safety of my operational laboratory.

It took me six more seconds to reach the bottom dark corner of the deserted laboratory where I had been projected into the future.

There were still almost 60 seconds left before my return time was set to energize and I knew if humans couldn't stand the sunlight that possibly the Paz Aliens would send ships to track me down.

Suddenly I could hear ships flying above and I knew that I was the purpose of their search.

Forty five more seconds to go and I curiously searched the dark corners of my former lab to see if anything was there to possibly help me survive the next few seconds until return activation.

I then remembered that in a storage closet near me there had been kept a led cloak garment for use in case of extreme radiation escape in the lab.

I quickly crawled on my hands and knees a few feet in the darkness feeling my way among familiar memories as the clock counted down to 20 more seconds before my return would energize.

I could hear a commotion in the stairwell of human voices in the distance as I figured that they had been transported here by Paz controlled ships.

I managed to get the locker door open and was surprised that the led shield garment was still there. I wondered if the led garment would shield my body from detection and I quickly in the dark put it on over myself and backpack which was counting steadily down to departure time.

Five seconds to go and I now cowered underneath in the corner ready to make a dash for the pedestal that I had arrived upon.

At 3 seconds I could hear human footsteps getting closer clanging on the metal stairway.

I quickly darted towards the pedestal that I was required to be on in order to return home.

Two seconds now and I could see flashlights bouncing off of the bunker walls as I ducked my head and waited for the backpack to energize and take me to my time of departure.

CHAPTER 15
HOME TO 2226

My last memory was of a guard energizing a laser towards my direction that passed right through me as I faded away through a swirling tunnel similar to the one that I had arrived to the future in.

I could still feel my burning skin from the hot sunlight that I had exposed myself to. It seemed as if minutes passed as I swirled backwards and then suddenly became aware of a east rotating Earth before Briana and lab assistants began rushing to the podium and helping me down to the laboratory's cool floor.

It was quickly ascertained that my skin was red with burns. Briana and lab technicians immediately transported me by a medical helicopter from the top floor to the hospital for emergency treatment of my exposed burns from the future's intense sunlight.

As I lay there for days recuperating in my hospital bed. My mind kept dwelling on what I had learned about the Paz and the future in the year 3000. No matter how hard I tried, I just couldn't stop thinking about the situation of the PAZ controlling all humans in the Ringworld's future.

It took my damaged body well over 30 days to heal to the point that I was able to get back to the research team and laboratory. I had been assured that the time machine apparatus was still operational and had been well maintained.

In the days that passed, I had briefed Briana and all of laboratory assistants of my perilous visit to the year 3000. All involved were astounded at the details that I had provided about how the Paz aliens ruled humans on the Ringworld and of details in the not too far away future.

I remembered how Paz had informed me that a message was sent into space from Earth in the year 2008. I surmised that if I could go back in time before that message was sent in the year 2008, that I could possibly change the future's outcome and prevent the Paz from ever receiving that message and coming here to conquer Earth.

Of course that was all conjecture but from what I had seen of the year 3000, I had to at least attempt to save humankind's destiny.

I had to at least try.

The entire staff got busy referencing Earth's history to somehow track down when and where that message had been sent from in the year 2008.

Finally after a month of research, the team had finally tracked the broadcast message down to an organization of that day called SETI which stands for search for extraterrestrial intelligence.

Historical research revealed that the message had been broadcast by SETI from a radio telescope located in a facility called Greenbank astronomy center in the state of West Virginia.

The specific message was broadcast at 10:45 PM on October 22nd in the year of 2008.

My staff and I also realized that our present facility underground did not exist in 2008 and the fact that we are now below the surface of the Earth, meant that I could possibly end up buried in below surface mud. That would be a problem if I were to reenergized in the same below surface coordinates that the laboratory existed at now before it was ever built.

That indeed was an unacceptable calculation that had to be solved before I could possibly consider transporting myself into the past in the year 2008.

Future Technologies facility was located on Earth's equator and Greenbank West Virginia was more than 38 degrees north above Earth's equator.

My early time machine had only been in its infancy stage of development. It had taken my staff and I three more months to be able to fine tune the time machine in order to send a time traveler to a specific coordinates at surface level.

It was an extreme necessity to be able to energize myself at a specific location on the surface of Earth. It was solved! The solution was that the Talaxia step down transformers had to be magnetically digitalized at the instant of transport to a specific microwave vibrating frequency.

This time I would be transporting to the past. Conditions had to be dealt with such as having an adequate amount of 2008 cash paper money on me in order to blend in with the current population of that time period.

In other words, you wouldn't want to use currency that was printed in the year of 2226. Different clothing of the era had to be considered also.

Yes indeed this would be an espionage attempt but something had to be done in an attempt to prevent that message from being broadcast into space.

No one of our century even knew if such an espionage attempt was even possible or not.

Our only option was to plan the espionage attempt and execute it to the best of our ability. The astronomers of 2008 had no idea of the consequences of what they did.

To SETI, the message was only a friendly gesture of peace beamed towards space.

I had to try to prevent the Paz from ever coming here to Earth. I had a deep desire to stop the PAZ from conquering humans. Humans deserve the right to determine their own destiny without alien interference.

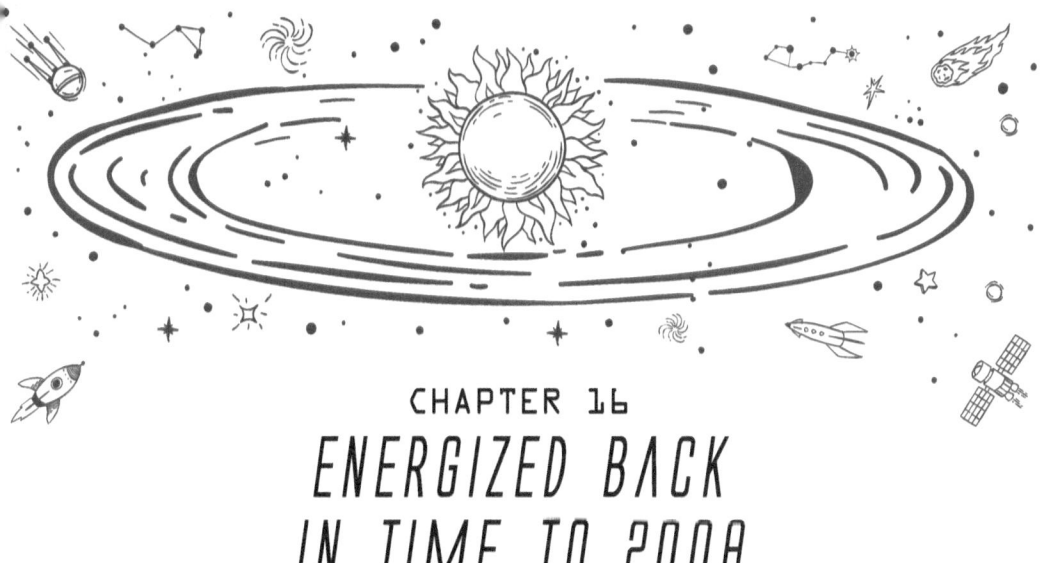

CHAPTER 16
ENERGIZED BACK
IN TIME TO 2008

It was late in November in my year of 2226 before all the perceived details had been dealt with and I, Irric Wapello again prepared to enter the time machine and attempt the espionage that would allow me to prevent the message of the past from being sent into space.

My backpack had been charged and it also contained many articles that I might need to accomplish the mission.

The backpack contained 30,000 dollars in cash of the period and also a laptop computer loaded with windows seven of that time period.

Also, I was equipped with a flying drone that had a laser weapon of my own time period's technology.

I remember thinking how curious the overall denim clothes that I was wearing were because the clothing of my present generation was so different than anything I was wearing now.

Present date was November 8th 2226.

I entered the time machine with my backpack equipped with all the things I would need to blend in to the West Virginia society that I would be dealing with once I arrived in the year 2008.

The time machine was set for me to arrive   just outside the small mountain community of Greenbank West Virginia on their exact time and date, of October the 8th, at 4 PM eastern standard time.

I was precisely set to be energized in a wooded area clearing a mile outside the edge of town on Highway 28 intentionally away from any possible early human contact.

This time, a shielded room had been installed around the transport podium.

I entered the blue walled room that Sunday morning at 8:15 AM, on my present time of November 8th, eastern standard time. I was equipped with my charged precious backpack loaded with all the necessities that I should need to accomplish my mission of sabotage.

As the time machine door closed behind my entrance, I suggested to Briana to set a countdown clock to begin at 60 seconds in order to prepare myself to sit perfectly still while the power was engaged to send me to the past.

I had been schooled on the ways of the past and had learned a lot about antique computers that existed in the year 2008.

Compared to computers of my time, these machine were obsolete.

Also, transport vehicles of my time, were mostly highway battery electric and the smog puffing gasoline vehicles of the past were memories of a hundred years ago.

The clock now counted down from 10 seconds as I positioned my body with backpack attached to remain extremely still when the count reached zero.

I heard the transformers power up and I watched the walls of the lab disappear as I began falling in a blue shifted tunnel towards years in the past before I was even born.

I could see below me through the tunnel walls a west rotating Earth spinning extremely fast before it began slowing to the time destination that I was to arrive at.

The blue walls of the tunnel now projected me towards a bright lit exit that turned shrubbery green as I found myself sitting in a clearing not far from a asphalt paved road just past a few tall pine trees to my right.

CHAPTER 17
ARRIVED MY DESTINATION

My first thoughts were to stand up immediately and ascertain the immediate situation that I had arrived in. Thirty seconds after I'd arrived, I could hear a dossier rumbling sound of a vehicle headed my way on the highway.

I quickly positioned myself far enough back into the wooded forest and concealed myself from the driver of the vehicles sight.

I had seen ancient videos of past earth vehicles but I have to admit that I was surprised at the noise that they made as they powered down the highway puffing poisonous gas fumes out the rear of their exhaust system.

Watching a video and experiencing ancient automobiles in real time was a different perspective to behold than what I had expected.

The vehicle that passed my concealed location was an older red Ford pick up truck with one person behind the steering wheel carrying a round bale of hay in the truck's bed.

Once the truck had passed, I exited the woods and started walking down the left side of the highway facing traffic towards the community of Greenbank West Virginia. I remember thinking to myself that if only the Henry Ford generation had known about putting magnets under the highway and also on the bottom of vehicles.

I walked on ahead facing sporadic oncoming traffic past a sign on the other side of the road that read Greenbank one mile.

At this point I realized that I was in the right place and it was now my duty to blend in to this society.

I was transported here in order to secretly perform my mission that was to be accomplished in two weeks time before the space message could be broadcast to the stars.

I certainly didn't even know if this mission was even possible but I was here to do it anyway.

It must have been about 5:45 pm when I managed to walk the mile distance to the edge of the community of Greenbank.

It was almost dusk and the sun was hanging low above the western horizon and the temperature had began dropping to cool thirty five degrees Fahrenheit.

I walked on along Highway 28 west and saw a sign up ahead on the left that read, Boyer Motel and Restaurant, reasonable rates.

Below the sign the vacancy sign was also lit.

I decided that this was as good of a place as any to begin my concealed mission.

CHAPTER 18
BOYER'S MOTEL

A tingling bell rang out as I opened the door to Boyer's Motel office.

The office appeared to be empty at first but shortly an elderly gentleman came out from a door behind the counter.

How you are today he spoke in his tone of mountain slang. Just fine Sir I replied. I hope you are fine as well.

I'd like to rent a room preferably around the back mountain facing side if possible I said.

I'm vacationing here in the area and I'll be here for two weeks

I was trying not to make significant eye contact as I spoke.

Well then he replied. Thar's a weekly rate of 350 dollars so, if you want the room for two weeks, that'll run you about 700 dollars plus tax. That'll make it a total of 742 dollars he replied with his mountain twang. You'll just need to fill out this registration form and show me your identification.

I presented the fake ID that I had been provided that showed that my name was Dalton Williams and that I was born in the Tallahassee Florida in the year 1981. I placed eight one hundred dollar bills on the counter and he seemed quite pleased that I paid the bill forward in cash money.

As I finished filling out the registration form he reached below the counter and pulled out a metal cash box and withdrew two twenties and a ten and eight one dollar bills as my change.

My name's Billy Clayton he said. My wife and I have run this motel for now on fifteen years.

The restaurant is open from 6AM till 8PM at night. Your room number will be 207 just up the stairs there and round ta the backside.

That's great Mr. Clayton I said. I thanked him and turned and headed towards the exit door with backpack attached and a key in hand with the number 207 on it.

Billy Clayton didn't seem to be suspicious of anything but before the door finished closing behind me he spoke out and said.

We'll be a changing the bed sheets every other day or so and we hope you enjoy your stay here at Boyer's Motel. Let us know ifin ya needs anything at all was his last words as I departed the office.

Everything had gone well so far and I'd arrived here safely on October the eighth in 2008. As I climbed up the metal stairway I just kept thinking that something seemed different than what I had expected of the era.

In my day, ground transportation was provided by almost silent electric vehicles that had to be charged on a regular basis.

I had seen videos of the era but I was completely surprised about just how this centuries automobiles and trucks produced noise and pollution as they moved along the highways.

I followed the short hallway to the backside of the motel and was impressed by the beauty of the sunset over the top of the mountain as I reached the room that I had rented for two weeks.

CHAPTER 19

ROOM 207

I had forgotten that it required a physical metal key to open the door in this era but after struggling for a few moments I managed to unlock the door to room 207.

The room had rose colored walls and a mirror that was hung slightly crooked over a chest of four drawers with a Bible in the top drawer.

The room had a single adequate bed with a not to clean shower but I considered it to be a safe enough place to stay and conduct my espionage mission in secrete.

At the end of the bed on a roller cart the room also had what I considered an ancient video device that was called a television set.

I exited out of my backpack and placed it on the floor beside the bathroom entrance and walked over to the video device trying to figure out how to operate the remote control to turn it on.

I figured it out shortly and the screen lit up with a political news broadcast of the current presidential election news of the day that was to take place in November next month.

I already knew the result of that upcoming election so I started scanning several channels to see what other videos of this era contained.

Not much really interested me on this television contraption so I shut it down after ten minutes and placed my backpack upon the bed and began sorting out all of the gadgets that I would need and I began planning my tomorrows first mission.

I had surmised that my first objective here was to provide myself with some sort of present day transportation.

I retrieved from my backpack the laptop computer that I had been issued. I called down to the main desk to get the motels pass phrase in order to log on to their internet provider.

Although I had training before I left about this ancient internet, it still took me several attempts to learn how to surf the web on this what I considered ancient computer's internet.

The first thing I tried on the windows 7 computer was to search local people that were trying to sell a vehicle that had a reasonable price.

I had been issued a fake drivers license with the identity of Dalton Williams that stated that I was born in Florida in the year 1981. I figured to remain anonymous it would be best if I didn't try to deal with a used car salesman that would probably ask me too many question about my reason for being here in Greenbank.

Before I retired for the night I had written down several addresses with vehicles for sale that I would investigate the next day.

CHAPTER 20

THE 1994 TOYOTA TERCEL

October the 9th, 2008.

I had left a wake up call for 7:00 AM this morning and was startled awake by the beeping of the room phone. I thanked Billy's wife Mrs. Gloria Clayton for the wake up call and removed the rest of my clothes. I then immersed myself under the warm waters of the shower. I whistled a tune while thinking deep of how to prepare myself for the days mission of finding personal transportation. It wasn't but a few minutes before I was dressed and out the door with thoughts of breakfast foremost on my mind.

My first impression of the motel's restaurant was that it was sufficient for most of my meals that I would need while I was here.

The restaurant layout consisted of five four people sized booths near the window and 8 barstools lined up in front of a counter with a cash register at the end.

I sat down alone in one of the booths and a pretty young waitress immediately came over with a menu and asked me if I wanted coffee.

Pinned to her shirt was the name of Melissa and I asked her what she recommended.

We have a special this morning of beacon eggs and sausage and a biscuit meal for 5.99 this morning she replied. Wow I thought to myself. In my time a meal like that would cost 20 dollars or more.

Trying not to appear conspicuous I replied, I'll have that then and that would be great. Melissa scribbled it down on her order pad and quickly turned to take an order from an elderly gentleman at the far end on a bar stool next to the register..

It wasn't long before I was served breakfast by the same waitress and I quietly consumed the meal I was served and asked for the bill so that I could begin my today's search for a vehicle.

I proceeded to the cashier and paid my bill and left a five dollar tip for the waitress that had served me. She seemed grateful for the tip.

The night before I had written down the phone number of a local taxi service and I saw that a pay phone existed in the corner of the restaurant.

I requested change for a dollar from Melissa the cashier and I proceeded to the dark corner to make my necessary calls to the seller and a call for a taxi to carry me to the address of a vehicle that I had written down the night before.

In 15 minutes a taxi pulled up to the front of the motel and I exited out to greet the male driver.

I gave him the address of a Joseph R. Jones at 114 old Route 28 Rd. That's where the add had said that Mr. Jones had a 1994 Black Toyota Tercel for sale and the asking price was eleven hundred dollars.`

I chatted with the friendly cab driver who said his name was Devin Carter as we rode along old highway 28. We talked about the weather and I told him that I was going to the address provided to look at a Toyota that was for sale.

I asked him if he would wait a while as I looked the car over when we arrived at the address.

Sure no problem Devin replied. Just remember the meter is running as I wait. Your time is my money he jested. No problem I replied. I'll be as fast as I can and pay you what ever is required.

It wasn't long before we approached a leaning brown mailbox with the numbers 124 on the left side of the road. Devin turned left and headed uphill on the rocky gravel half mile long rough road that finally led up to an old frame house on top of a hill at the driveways dirt path end.

Earlier I had called the owners number before I had left my room and told him my name and that I was coming by to look at the Toyota that he had for sale.

At the top of somewhat shaky steps, there stood and older gentleman smoking a pipe as the taxi pulled up in his front yard.

I assumed that was Mr. Jones as I exited the cab.

Hello there Mr. Jones I said as I approached the wooden steps that he was at the top of.

Sir. I'm Dalton Williams and I called you earlier about the Toyota for sale.

How-do he replied as he began hobbling down the old wooden steps while holding the smoking pipe in his mouth and clutching onto the wooden railing.

The car is around back of the house he said. You'd better give me a minute to tie up my old Dawg Ginseng before you wander around thar to take a look at the car he said. He's a bit cantankerous round strangers sometimes. Only thang he's good fer is sniffing out wild ginseng.

I recon I'll be back in a few minutes he said. You wait right thar until I come back. Okay I said. I'll wait.

In five minutes Mr. Jones returned to the corner of the house and motioned me forward.

The old houses siding looked worse than the front appeared but we pushed ahead uphill until we came to the backside where the car sat that he wanted to sell.

The roof was faded black in color but the rest of the paint had a hidden shine to it. The car could definitely use a wash job. Evidently it had been sitting a while and accumulated a lot of West Virginia dust. Why are you selling the car I asked. I looked him in the eye and realized that Mr. Jones seemed emotional about the question I'd asked.

This car was my only son Kinlow's car he answered with a raspy voice. He lost his life over thar in the Iraq war in 2006. I was sorry I had asked now that I was seeing the stress in Mr. Jones response. I'm so sorry for your loss I replied. The car's been setting thar for now on two years Mr. Jones stated.

I opened the door and fumbled around until I found the hood release. The inside was a bit dirty but that didn't concern me.

I closed the door and raised the hood to check the oil level and several other fluids before I decided to ask Mr. Jones if I could hear the engine run.

Sho nuff can he responding as he handed me a single key to start the engine. Same key fits the boot too he said.

For the first time I realized that it was a stick shift and I had never driven a automobile that I had to shift gears before. I turned the switch hard to the right and nothing happened.

You gotta mash in on the clutch afore she'll start Mr. Jones hollered after he saw that I was having trouble starting the car.

Ok I replied thinking to myself. Now, what the heck is a clutch. There was no such thing in my century and this was one of the things that I had not been made aware of in my training.

Finally I asked Mr. Jones to come over and start the car for me while I got out and pretended to be inspecting the tires on the passenger side.

I watched closely through the passenger window as he sat in the car and pushed the far left pedal all the way to the floorboard and then twisted the key and the car's starter engaged and the motor began running.

Mr. Jones chuckled as he exited the car and said, you city boys must not be familiar with a standard transmission.

No sir I responded. I'm not familiar with that type of gears in a car. How does it work I asked.

He looked at me a bit concerned. Well, the gears are first ,second, third and fourth and the gear stick is laid out in a H pattern. In the middle line of the H pattern is Neutral.

You start off in first gear releasing the clutch slowly at the top left of the H pattern. Once you git yerself a going ya then push the clutch down and move the stick straight back to the bottom left side of the H pattern for second gear.

Then, third gear is to the top right of the H pattern and fourth gear is straight back of the right side of the H pattern and that's the gear that you use when you're going down the highway at top speed.

Oh he said , after you release the clutch slowly and start off in first gear, you use the clutch between each gear you change to and always when you come to a stop.

How do you back up I asked. Oh he said, You first put the stick in the neutral line position and push it down and hard over to the right and then ya pull back to the right of the forth gear position to achieve reverse gear.

You sure that you have a license he squinted his brow when asking.

Yes Sir I replied. I've just never driven a car with a transmission of this kind.

I tell you what Mr. Jones replied back. Ifin you decide to buy the car for eleven hundred dollars cash, I'll drive you down to the local DMV office and show you how the gears work on the way to get the title changed into your name.

You'll have to bring me back home though after we've completed the deal. That sounds great I replied. I really would appreciate you doing that for me. It's a deal then I stated and pulled out eleven one hundred dollar bills and placed them in his right hand.

I paid the taxi driver a thirty five dollar fee and sent him on his way while Mr. Jones went in his house to retrieve the title to the car that I had just purchased.

Mr. Jones came down his front steps carrying a green paper title in his right hand and handed it to me and told me to hang on to it until we arrive at the DMV.

You'd better let me drive he said. I'll show you how to drive a standard transmission on the way. I got in the passenger side and he got behind the wheel of the black Toyota Tercel.

He showed me the H patter of the stick shift and showed me also the neutral stick position and how to put the car in reverse.

He explained to me that once the motor was running you had to push the clutch in to put the stick in first gear and release it slowly until the car was moving about 10 miles per hour. Then, you push the clutch in again and move the stick to the second gear position and speed up until about 25 mph. Then you push the clutch in and move the stick to third gear position and speed up to about 40 mph and do the same thing for the fourth gear until you reach top speed or ever how fast you want to go in forth gear.

It all seemed a bit confusing in my mind but I kept my words to myself as I silently observed Mr. Jones as he continued to drive us to the local DMV office.

It took about 20 minutes to arrive at the DMV and I watched as Mr. Jones pulled into the parking lot and parked. He then pulled the center stick hand brake up and shut the engine off with a left twist of the key.

That's all thar is to it he said. I think I understand it now I replied as we both exited the Toyota and headed for the DMV office door.

Inside the DMV I was surprised that I couldn't register the car into my name unless I changed my drivers license to a West Va. address.

The DMV did allow me to do that after I gave them my address of the motel that I was staying at.

There was a title charge, and a notary and tax fees that had to be paid and a fee for the license plate that I was purchasing for the Toyota. The total bill was over 165 dollars for all of the title change taxes and license plate.

I also had to purchase car insurance from an agent that was conveniently set up inside the DMV. The car insurance cost me another 250 hundred dollars for six months.

Mr. Jones stuck with me all through the registration process. I considered him to be a very nice man.

I could have never received that kind of help had I purchased a car from a used car lot. I was very thankful for his help.

We left the DMV and went outside with my new license plate and registration in my hands and Mr. Jones opened the trunk and retrieved a screw driver and began removing his old license plate and began installing the new plate that was registered to myself.

Upon completion he stood up and handed me the key and said, all right Mr. Williams, It's your turn to drive. It's your car now as he entered the passenger side and fastened his seat belt.

I was a bit nervous as I climbed behind the steering wheel to attempt to drive the black 94 Toyota Tercel that I had just purchased.

With a twist of the key while holding the clutch in, the car started promptly and I released the hand brake and pushed the gear stick into first gear. I let the clutch out too fast and the engine chocked off and I had to restart the Toyota. You have to release the clutch slowly when you starting off in first gear Mr. Jones instructed.

After another attempt I managed to get the hang of it and learned the process of operating a standard transmission. I only forgot once at a stop light that I had to always push the clutch in while sitting still with the motor running.

In another 20 minutes I'd arrived at Mr. Jones's home and he got out and stated that he wished me good luck with the Toyota that he had sold me. Wait I said as he began to leave the car, I handed him another 50 dollars and said, that's for all the help that you gave me at the DMV and teaching me how to operate a standard transmission. I really do appreciate it I said.

Well thank you thar Mr. Williams said and I appreciate you being so kind in purchasing this old Toyota. I think you'll get good service out of er. I hope that yall have a good day he stated as he wandered toward his front steps while striking a match to light his pipe again as he walked away.

That was the last time that I ever saw Mr. Jones and that by the time I had completed the car purchase that day and carried him back home, the time was 4:35 PM when I drove back to my room at the motel.

I had been nervous the whole day thinking that I might be discovered and all my espionage plans to stop the message from being broadcast would have ended in vain.

I had left the backpack in my room and if anything had gone wrong I would have had no way of immediate escape from this century.

I entered my room and everything seemed normal. I was so glad to get back to what I considered safety and solitude. I had a slight headache from the days episode of buying the Toyota which I was to use in the coming days of my reason for being here in this century.

It wasn't long before I had stretched out on the bed and took a long nap to relieve the stress of the day. I must have fell into rim sleep because I dreamed about the evil Paz and all the chaos they had caused to the humans of the future. I awoke at 4:30 AM October 10th refreshed but aware of the bad dream I had about the Paz.

I turned this centuries version of entertainment on and let it play while I showered and changed clothes for this days journey once the sun had risen.

CHAPTER 21

DAY TWO IN GREENBANK

The clothes I pulled from my backpack were a bit humorous to me as I examined the denim material that the jeans were made from.

T shirts and socks were different also because in my century people wore synthetic material clothing.

At 6:15 AM, I was one of the first customers to enter the motel diner that morning. There was one elderly gentleman sitting on a stool at the far end of the bar.

The same waitress Melissa headed my way carrying a cup in her left hand and the hot coffee pot in her right hand.

Good morning she said. What will it be this morning she asked.

She stared at me curiously as I sat there a moment without responding to her. Oh, I finally replied as she began pouring the coffee in the mug.

I'll have that same special that I had yesterday. Okay then she replied scribbling on her order pad. Sausage bacon eggs and a biscuit coming up and she quickly returned towards the order window tacking the paper slip to a metal pin wheel in the opening to the kitchen.

About 5 minutes later Melissa returned carrying my plate of breakfast food.

I was trying to stay silent but something about Melissa intrigued me. I noticed that she was wearing a wedding ring but I decided to ask her last name as she sat the plate of food down softly on the table. She didn't reply because several other customers entered and she turned and hurried to take their orders.

I watched as she rushed to pin their orders to the kitchen window and as soon as she had done that several other patrons joined the early morning breakfast rush.

I ate my breakfast and sipped the last of my coffee and got up from my meal and headed to the cash register to pay my bill. Melissa rushed over and rang my total up as 6 dollars and 42 cents and she politely said sorry that I didn't answer you before but my last name is Harris. Oh Okay, I replied. No problem. I was just curious because I've been coming in here the past couple of mornings and I always see you working so hard.

Well then It's nice to know your whole name and I'm Dalton Williams and I handed her a 12 dollars and told her to keep the change. Thanks a lot she replied I really appreciate the tip. You're welcome I said and I turned and exited the restaurant and walked around behind the motel where I had parked the Toyota that I'd purchased the day before.

I decided that it's time to get in the Toyota and do a little research exploration of the job that I would need to accomplish in a few days.

Now that I understood the concept of this four speed standard transmission, I had become quite efficient at changing the gears and using the clutch.

This day I drove up and down highway 28 exploring the immediate area and decided it was time to pull in and gas up the car at a self service gasoline pump.

This was my first time at actually smelling gasoline because in my century most of the ground vehicles that I knew about were all electric even though they did have to be plugged in to a recharger.

I filled the tank and after spending about 21 dollars on gasoline, I decided to drive up to what was called telegraph road where the entrance to the Greenbank telescope was located.

The telescope itself was barely visible from the entrance because it was behind a band of trees and was a kilometer past the guard house up a paved road.

I didn't enter the road because I didn't want to project any suspicion for the future days.

I had to prepare myself mentally to disable the telescope at the proper time needed.

I did drive slowly past the telegraph road entrance the first time trying to see what had to be dealt with when it was time to perform my espionage act on the 22nd of October. That time was a little over 11 days away.

The next seven days I did all I could to investigate the security of the Greenbank telescope complex. I had discovered a dirt path a mile or so past the guarded entrance that led way back into the woods.

On the seventh day I investigated the unpaved dirt path that ended up at a dead end creek that I estimated was approximately a half mile behind where the telescope was located.

Everything went well and I decided that this would be a good place to launch the drone that I had brought with me from the future.

In the year 2008, drones were just beginning to be utilized and the technology wasn't very sophisticated. The drone that I had brought with me from my century, was very sophisticated in comparison to 2008 present technology.

My drone was equipped with stealth ability and a powerful laser that was very powerful and could easily cut through wires from as far as a quarter mile away.

My drone was also equipped with infrared vision to be able to see in the dark.

The windows 7 laptop that I'd brought with me from the future, had to be calibrated to be able to work with the drone of the future that I would deploy at the proper time.

Also, the laptop itself had to be upgraded to 1 Terabyte of random access memory which would seem very strange in this year of 2008 because computers didn't have that much Ram capabilities yet in this time period.

The extra ram was required to fly the futuristic drone that I was to use to disable the telescope when the proper time came on the night of October 22nd.

The next ten days passed as I continuously investigated the dirt path that led to the creek to see if any service vehicles ever used the path that I was to use on my espionage night attempt.

I never once say a vehicle go up or depart that dirt path in my investigation over ten days time.

All had gone well for the past days and I had become a regular in the area and especially the motel restaurant.

TWO DAYS TO GO

It was now the evening of October the 20'th and I had finished my meal of steak, potatoes and macaroni and cheese that evening as the sun was setting on the western horizon.

I was two nights away from my attempt to disable the Greenbank Radio Telescope and as soon as it was good and dark, this night's plan was to drive down the dirt path and test out the drone that I had from my centuries technology.

I left the restaurant about dusk and headed up the stairs to my room to retrieve my backpack and checked the power status of my return power condenser that was my only way to get back to my century.

A hour or so had passed and when everything that I needed was checked out I decided it was time to load the backpack in the trunk of the Toyota and head past the Greenbank Telescope complex entrance and sneak in the dark into the dirt path that led to the creek about a half mile in the woods behind where the telescope was actually located.

There wasn't any traffic at night on highway 28 as I drove out of the motel lot at 8:30 PM and headed west on 28 until after about 8 kilometers I slowly passed by the entrance to the road that led to the telescope complex.

As I passed the entrance to Telescope road,

I took an extra long look at the closed guard shack and noticed that the gate was closed and everything looked peaceful and perfectly normal.

Another one and a half kilometers in the darkness ahead I could see the path coming up on the right where I was to turn in and travel back behind the telescope to the creek.

As soon as I turned down the dirt path I turned off the lights and drove real slow trying to make as little noise as possible.

I knew that if I were to get caught back here at the creek that I would probably get arrested and then my mission could not be accomplished.

The black color of the Toyota was helpful in concealing my presence as I came to a stop at the paths end near some bushes that lead down to the creek.

As silently as I could, I got out and opened the trunk and got the backpack out and spread the contents out on the hood of the Toyota.

Everything was quite and very dark. There was no moon out tonight and as I assembled the drone the only sounds heard were the crickets and night sounds of animals in the forest.

Now the drone that I was assembling was not from this century It was from mine. Before departure from my century technicians had gone to great lengths to improvise this special drone to work through a windows 7 operating system from the lap top that I had brought with me to the past.

I unpacked the special folding visor that enabled me to operated the drone that I was about to launch in tonight's test.

With the drone assembled I put on the inflatable virtual reality control visor on my head that allowed me to fly the drone with the help of the computer.

I set the drone on the top of the black Toyota and engaged the visor's power that lit up in the darkness a stealth green color.

The face shield displayed the infrared camera view that could see extremely well in the darkness of the area.

This futuristic drone that I was using had very unique features and abilities. Also the head gear that I was wearing projected a green infragreen shield around my body when activated that would prevent anyone from seeing me unless they were as close as ten feet away.

The drone itself could fly in a super silent mode that no one could possibly hear. The drone also had the same cloaking field around it so that it would appear invisible to anyone that was looking in the direction that it was flying or hovering.

No radar of this centuries technology could possibly detect it. In the darkness of the area that I was launching the drone from, the only thing visible at the moment was the black Toyota itself and in the no moon lit sky, even the black Toyota was very hard to see.

In the cloaked darkness of this October 20th night I began booting up the windows 7 computer and shielded the screen under my helmet visor and activated the infrared camera and engaged the drones silent mode as it lifted from the top of the car.

There was a slight distorted blur as it moved above the tree tops but to the eye it was almost impossible to detect in the night sky.

CHAPTER 23
SNAKE SCARE

As I was concentrating on the cloaked computer screen, I felt something brush around my right pants leg and I looked down and screamed out loud in fright as I discovered that a 6 feet snake had began wrapping itself around my right ankle denim pant leg.

I was so terrified that I jumped away from the car and slung the drone's visor controller from my face to the ground while kicking the large snake away and off my leg as I ran away from the car.

I had kicked the snake away from me that had started to wrap itself around my right ankle just in time to prevent it from closing up around my leg.

I was so scared in the moment that I had completely momentarily forgotten that I had launched the drone and had detached the control visor from my face and tossed it to the ground as I ran away.

In the meantime the snake had slithered underneath the Toyota and it took me a minute or so to even gather my thoughts and courage to grab the visor a few feet away from me.

I quickly grabbed the control visor and set it on auto pilot while I eased my way back to the car and opened the driver side door and immediately set the laptop that was on top of the car in the passenger seat. I then jumped in and started the Toyota and moved it 50 feet away from where it had been before the snake incident had occurred.

As I got out of the car I witnessed the tail of the snake crawling back into the brush.

My heart was still beating fast from the encounter but I soon managed to set the laptop up again and continued my test of the drone system.

The drone was hovering on auto pilot about 300 feet high just past the tree line. I released the auto pilot and began directing it towards the area where the telescope was located.

The night vision clocking device allowed me to have an excellent view of the night sky and ground area below. Since this was only a test I decided that I would fly the drone in a circle to orbit the telescope once to see if any alarms went off and then direct it back to the location that I was at approximately a half mile away.

The drone approached the telescope silently in a cloaking mode and lowered itself to the height of the large dish array and hovered momentarily. Then the drone began a slow rotation of the huge dish. No alarms sounded so I decided to take a picture before directing it back to my location.

Other than the snake incident, everything went well that night of the test. No one seemed to detect that the drone had even visited the Greenbank Telescope.

I move the laptop to the side and the drone sat down silently on top of the car and I began packing up all of the equipment getting ready to depart the area.

That Monday night of October the 20th I managed to get back to my room about 11:20 PM still thinking about how lucky I had been with the snake encounter and the test flight of the drone that had went well.

I suppose it was the snake encounter that caused me to have a bad dream that night. But even so, I awoke the next morning content on what I had accomplished the night before.

I had also proven to myself that the area was safe to conduct my espionage of the telescope on Wednesday the 22nd.

That Tuesday morning I showered and got dressed and headed down to the restaurant for a hearty breakfast. I was glad to see that Melissa

Harris was my waitress again and took my order and brought me my meal with a pleasant attitude.

She seemed a bit friendlier this morning asking me my name again and questioning me about my stay here in Greenbank.

I told her how much I liked the beauty and serenity of the area and let her know that my stay here was almost over and that I would be leaving in a couple of days.

I suppose since I was a good tipper she seemed sad that I was leaving and wished me luck on my journey home and told me she hopped that I would come back here again sometime.

Directly, she started to hurry off to wait on other customers that had just arrived but before she did I reminded her of my name and informed her that after tomorrow that I would be heading home.

In my mind I was thinking to myself that if only she knew what I really meant by heading home. If only she really knew the truth I thought to myself with a chuckle.

All of that Tuesday I mostly hung around my room trying to stay as inconspicuous as possible.

I was kind of bored with the political news of the day and I suppose that was because I already knew my history and the results of the current political election.

I was really fascinated by the old western movie that I was watching about the gold rush days of the late eighteen hundreds.

I went to the car after dark and retrieved my backpack to recheck the status of my equipment and the charged capacitor that stored the energy to get me back to my century when the proper time arrived after the espionage of the Greenbank Telescope was completed.

Everything seemed to be in order with all the equipment so I crawled into bed that Tuesday the 21st content that everything should go fine with tomorrow nights disabling of the telescope.

If anything did go wrong tomorrow night it would allow the telescope technicians to broadcast a message that would cause great harm to the future. If only they knew the truth. I had to stop that transmission. That's all there is to it.

If only there had been a way that I could have told someone that would possibly believe me. That wasn't an option. No one from this date in time would believe time travel was even possible.

CHAPTER 24
ESPIONAGE NIGHT

October the 22nd, 2008.

I awoke about 7 AM with extreme optimism about accomplishing my mission tonight. I showered and dressed and hurried down to have my normal breakfast at the motel restaurant. Melissa was there as usual and cheerfully waited on me just like most mornings.

We exchanged a few pleasantries and before I knew it my breakfast was setting before me as she scurried away back towards the kitchen.

Through the window to the front I observed two West Virginia state police cars pull into the parking lot. I assumed they were just here to get breakfast but I certainly didn't need any problems with the police.

I ignored them as they came inside and sat on the bar stools and gave Melissa their orders. I noticed one of them did turn and look around the room but all seemed normal as I got up and went to the cashier to pay my bill.

One of the officers turned and looked my way. He did look me over but then turned and started talking to the officer beside him.

Melissa came to the register and took my money and again I gave her a five dollar tip and thanked her for her service.

As I exited the restaurant the other officer turned and looked my way momentarily but didn't say anything as I walked by him.

I was a bit paranoid that they had both took the time to look me over but all things considered I didn't think much about it anymore once

I had returned to my room to spend time planning tonight's attempt at disabling the telescope.

I spent most of the daylight in my room but about 2 PM I decided to drive to a local Walmart. I wasn't planning on buying anything inside so basically I just sat there for an hour listening to the news broadcast on the car radio.

I did very much enjoy watching the girls scurry in and out with wobbly wheeled baskets of food products and cleaning products with the children tagging close behind their mothers.

In this century, I was becoming amazed at peoples actions and reactions in a Walmart parking lot. Long thoughts in the Toyota reminded me of my purpose. Here, humans had free will.

If my espionage tonight were to fail, human beings of future generations would lose their freedom and their free will.

I had to win. My timer beeped at 3:40 PM bringing me back to reality. I turned off the radio and twisted the key and bumped the starter and the Toyota Tercel came to life.

I was back to my room about 4:15 PM and waited another hour or so just before dusk to load up my backpack and other equipment that I would need.

Back in my room I waited to around 8 PM that night to get in the Toyota to begin the important task that I had come to this century to do. It was indeed the most important thing I had ever attempted in my life.

My reasoning was that if I could stop the message being transmitted tonight, that I could possibly save humans future and prevent the Paz from ever conquering Earth.

It wasn't only important to myself, it was important to the entire planet's future population.

CHAPTER 25
IT'S NOW OR NEVER

Around 8:30 PM, I turned the Toyota Tercel to the right that led into the back road behind the Greenbank Telescope Facility.

It was getting darker by the minute as the dusk light was well past the western sunset.

I parked the car in the place that I had moved to after the snake encounter and began setting up the laptop and drone on top of the Toyota.

I put the cloaking drone controller over my head and energized the power source.

The message was recorded to be sent at 10:45 PM this night of October 22nd, 2008.

I didn't want to disable the telescope too early because it may give the technicians time to repair the wires and send the message anyway.

I had more plans than to just cut the wires. I needed to make sure it was days or even months before they could accomplish repairs.

Thirty five minutes passed with only the night sounds could be heard.

At 9:58 PM, The drone lifted up from the top of the Toyota in it's cloaking mode.

I stood among the dark wooded area oblivious to all other moments in time.

The drone soared past the tree tops and headed due north towards the telescope target.

Through the visor projection, I had excellent night vision capability and could see the huge telescope getting closer by the minute.

The drone cleared the tree tops and hovered low on its way across the open field where the telescope existed.

I piloted the drone to fly five feet above ground level and slowly approached the lower base of the radio telescope.

I hovered the drone at the lower structure fuse box for sixty seconds or so while I visually inspected the wiring from below ground connected to the fuse box that was powering the telescope.

The laser energized and began cutting through both of the 2 inch diameter lower feed wires.

Sparks sprayed the area as the wires were being cut in half.

I knew then that somebody would notice and come to investigate. But the control room itself was a good distance away from the telescope.

The lower wires cut I now zoomed the drone up to where the upper wires were and quickly began cutting those wire that led to the transmitter in the center.

Just as I finished cutting both sets of wires, the entire area lit up with powerful search lights to investigate the intrusion.

I spotted headlights approaching the area as I began to activate the remaining deactivation surprise from the drone.

The drones ability of finale assault was also equipped with an implosion device. When dropped from above the telescope by the drone, the small implosion device would cause the center telescope's projection point to fall inward and totally disable the radio telescope for many days.

I released the implosion device and watched as it struck dead center making a huge sucking sound as the center projection tower fell to the middle of the telescope with a metallic sounding crash.

It was done. I immediately directed the drone to return to my location and after several minutes it landed softly on top of my Toyota.

It was 10:43 PM when I quickly began packing up all of my equipment and in 3 minutes time, I was sitting behind the wheel ready to depart the area.

I drove lights out along the dark path and I managed to get back to the main road without detection. I turned right and headed away from Greenbank and drove a good 15 minutes before I decided to turn around and attempt to get back to my room without getting captured.

On my return I passed the access road to the left where I launched the attack.

As I drove by, there was one state trooper vehicle entering the path to the woods.

I kept driving and as I passed the entrance to the telescope facility it was all lit with lights and several other police vehicles were on the scene with police lights rolling.

I was scared. I just knew that one of those police cars would come after me since I was the only vehicle to pass by the area headed towards Greenbank.

My main objective now was to get back to the area a mile outside of town and activate the energy compacitor in order to return to my century. There was no need in going back to the motel. Job accomplished, my mission now was to get home.

I drove the Toyota past the motel and headed west on highway 28. The place I had to get to was just past the Greenbank one mile sign that I saw when I first arrived.

Approaching the area I quickly pulled the Toyota over to the right and got out and opened the trunk to put on my backpack.

I could see and hear a vehicle coming fast down the highway. I threw the straps across my shoulders and ran in the woods as fast as I could to get to the location where I could activate the stored energy power pack that would get me home.

I could see through the brush as a state troopers pulled behind and another in front of the now abandoned Toyota. In the darkness beside the Toyota they had activated all of their patrol lights.

Cowering beside a bush I could see two humans moving around in the lights past the trees.

The last thing I remember seeing and hearing was a voice from a officer ordering me to come out of the woods with my hands over my head.

My finger was on the activation key and I pushed the control button to activate the return device.

The officers must have thought they were seeing things as I faded away into nothingness and fell through the time tunnel back to my own century of late 2226. To this day, I always wondered who would be the next person to buy that Toyota Tercel.

CHAPTER 26
RETURNED HOME TO THE LAB

Tumbling trough jelly-mist waves inside the purple lit walls of a waterfalls glory and spiraling always forward and to the right, I now could visualize a far away view of the planet earth spinning swiftly to the east of its north pole. Seconds passed as the Earth grew closer in late November 2226.

I materialized in light at first then to solid matter on the podium in front of Briana and the laboratory team. I was slightly disoriented for a moment but I quickly became fully aware of where I was and the situation that I'd left behind in Greenbank West Virginia.

My backpack was intact and all the recorded information was there to be retrieved and stored in the present day archives.

By early December of 2226 all the facts had been revealed of my journey and further plans were being made for a future trip back to the year 3000 to see if any results had changed and see if the Paz was there and still in control of humanities fate.

Knowing what I had experienced before in the 30th century, this time when I returned, I was planning to be way better prepared than I was the first time that I'd visited the future.

It was decided at the laboratory that we would take a short break and allow the holidays to pass before any attempt would be made before I would be transported back to the year 3,000.

Meticulous plans were being made though in order to make the transport happen on January 6th 2227.

CHAPTER 27
I'VE GOT TO KNOW!

I have to know the real truth. Did My Espionage in the past work? I'm going back to find out the truth. That's all there is to it.

It was the first of the year in 2227 before we all gathered in the Lab on January 5th.

We began by going over all the details of the next mornings transport. No one knew whether or not anything would be changed in the future but we had extreme knowledge of what the situation was that occurred before.

For instance, we knew that the sun's rays would burn you and if the Paz were there and still in control, we had to improvise a way to conceal me from the Paz's ability to read my thoughts.

This time, I would be allowed to carry a weapon and use a cloaking device to hide my thoughts from being discovered. I could also make my backpack invisible in order to hide it if it became necessary.

We were all hoping that preventing the message from being sent in 2008 would change the future and possibly humanity would again control its own destiny.

The truth is, we had no way of knowing what the situation was. The only sure way to find out the truth, was to go back to 3000 and see.

I did have some idea that this time maybe I would be a little better prepared to deal with any situation that might occur.

January 6th, 2227 9:45 AM,

I, Irric Wapello sat there on the transporter as ready as I could possible be.

I do have to admit that I was a bit scared but curiosity cured any fear that I had.

I was ready to face the future again and see if the situation was different than what I had experienced on my earlier voyage to the year 3000.

CHAPTER 28
ENERGIZED TO 3000

I gave Briana the thumbs up to let her know that I was ready to be launched into the future.

It's really hard to explain the feeling of being dematerialized and still being conscious of your present state of being.

As I tumbled and swirled through long curvy tunnels, I sensed a strange feeling of pulling and stretching of the atoms in my own body as I traveled.

It wasn't as if the atoms were being pulsed in and out apart. It was if atoms in my cells were the consistency of jello and were being stretched and contracted in pulses as I fell towards the future.

The illuminated earth at the tunnels end was in sight and before I knew it, I again sat materialized in the dark former lab that once was our headquarters in my past.

I took a few seconds to orient myself and reached for a flashlight that I had stored in my backpack before departure from my century.

The readout on my backpack said that the date was April the 2nd in the year 3,000.

The underground lab appeared the same as it did the first time that I had arrived in this century. I had no idea yet as to what the situation was above. I began crossing the floor and heading towards the left and where the stairwell was located.

I began climbing the cobwebbed stairs as I did when I visited this century before. As I got nearer to the top I could hear sounds that I couldn't quite yet identify.

It sounded more like air rushing or gushing louder then receding away with the dossier effect.

I was one flight of stairs away from the top as the swishing sounds grew louder. To my surprise as I stepped to the top floor's exit, there were flying vehicles moving a foot above a magnetic paved highways. I thought out loud to myself, If only early society had put magnets below the roadways when cars were first invented, there would never have been any need for gasoline powered polluting vehicles. If so, Earth's air would have been protected from pollution in the past centuries.

I knew right away that this was not the future I had visited before. Something definitely had changed. There were elevated round homes offset along the highways that resembled saucer shapes with solar windows all around.

I watched as one human exited his home and got inside an arrow shaped vehicle and descended down to the green lawn then moved methodically towards the highway and instantly connected to an invisible U shaped magnetic field and zoomed away in the opposite direction that I stood.

Wow I thought. Evidently my trip to the past had caused a big difference in this century.

These were humans flying above ground vehicles and everyone seemed to have a purpose in their destinations.

The ring system high above the planet was still there but the breathable air was way fresher than it was before.

The giant pylon columns supporting the ring system were colored gold and the closest one that I had visited in my earlier voyage was reflecting sunlight with a bright golden reflection.

No one seemed to notice me as I stood in a field on top of the abandoned underground research lab that had once been my starting point.

Vehicles swished by above the highway continuously at speeds that I estimated at approximately 250 kilometers per hour. I was totally amazed at the difference this future represented so far.

There were indeed many more facts to learn about this changed century. At this point my only option was to walk along side the highway towards the pylon 21 that I had visited before and see if I would be allowed to be a welcomed visitor.

According to my daylight time measurer, it was 11:30 AM on April the 2nd in this century. The sky was blue and the sun was high over head causing the rings above to produce a shadowy projection slightly off center from the rings high over head structure.

I began walking along beside the highway towards the pylon 21 support that I had visited on my first journey here. Pylon 21 was the same distance away but the gold surface color was definitely different than before.

Vehicles swished by as I walked along but no one seemed to pay any attention to me.

There were other humans in their yards as I walked past their homes. One even waved to me as I passed his location. I stopped and walked over to ask him how he was and he was curious about the backpack that I wore and asked me if I was a camper. I fibbed and told him that I was and began a conversation about the ring system high over our head.

He introduced himself as Jason Miller and told me that the ring system was built in 2795 and was very curious that I didn't know that. Oh I replied that I did know that but was curious as to who was in charge of it now.

He replied that the military was in charge and was very perplexed as to why I didn't know that fact either. Well Sir I told him, that I had been away visiting relatives that lived in Greenland and had just returned to this area a short time ago and that I figured that the military was in charge but I was just asking to make sure that was still the case.

We exchanged a few more pleasantries and I told him my name was Dalton Williams and started walking away from his yard towards pylon

21. He looked at me strangely as I departed and when I looked back he was entering his home as if nothing unusual had occurred.

I walked again towards the huge gold column and in thirty minutes I had arrived at the back side. Again I proceeded to follow the columns round circumference and in another twenty minutes I approached the northside entrance to column 21's front round door.

So far the only difference to the column was its color but the number 21 had a military insignia of an eagle above the number 21.

The touch pad was still there at the right side of the round door so I proceeded to enter the same numbers that I had entered before which was 3.14.

As I did just as before an alarm sounded and the door silently rolled to the left. To my surprise this time a robotic creature floated out to greet me speaking first in a language that I was not familiar with. I didn't understand a word it was transmitting to me so I spoke in English my name as it hesitated and began translating to the english language.

You have no ID badge it said. You are not allowed here. Get away it commanded and then turned and quickly returned behind the closing rolling door. The best way that I can describe the robot is that it was deep blue in color and a meter diameter ball shape that hovered several feet above the ground and the voice it used was mechanical in nature.

Except for telling me to get away, it hadn't threatened me in anyway.

What the heck I thought. I had come a long way and wasn't about to be dissuaded that quickly.

I punched the numbers in again. Nothing happened. So I decided to reverse the numbers to 41.3 and try again.

The door slid open this time and a much larger round robot floated out and without word lassoed me with an electric force field and literally drug me inside the complex and pinned me up against the inside wall.

It's command was forceful and direct telling me to surrender my backpack and if I moved I would be destroyed.

I was shocked and unable to do anything but comply to its command. Again I was disarmed from my backpack and literally guided into a containment cell without out further words.

CHAPTER 29

DETAINED AGAIN IN 3000

The entire inside complex had many different sized robots that moved around with self determined priorities. The fact that I was a human didn't seem to phase any of the robots at all.

I was detained in my cell for several hours before a human exited the elevator and walked towards my cell.

This human was a female officer that walked up to my cell and spoke in what appeared to another foreign dialect that I didn't understand. When I spoke to her in English her faced showed a surprised expression and she began speaking back to me in my language. She first demanded to know my name and asked who I was and then wanted to know where I had originated from.

I decided to be truthful and not conceal my identity as I had the first time that I visited the year 3000.

I began telling her the facts of my journey here earlier and explained the details of my 2008 time trip and she began looking at me like I was totally insane.

The female officer identified herself as Officer Calamander Johnson and she ordered me abruptly to shut my mouth and that she insinuated that I was a liar.

She immediately discharged her weapon and laserjected into my veins some sort of truth serum that caused me to immediately tell her the same truth that I had just told her before the injection.

You must be immune to the truth injector she replied with a bit of anger. I'll need to report this incident to the high commander she snarled my way.

She turned without further interrogation and retreated back to the elevator that she had arrived in.

So Far, She had been the only human contact inside on this lower floor of pylon 21. I watched her in her retreat as she passed by many different sized robots busy at a task that I couldn't yet identify.

Another hour passed and this time she returned with another male officer that started interrogating me with a rude vengeance.

This male officer wanted to know how I was able to evade the truth weapon. Then he again laserjected the side of my head. He hadn't even bothered to tell me his identity but I assumed by his elaborate shoulder decorations that he was a higher ranked officer and had more authority to find out exactly who I was.

I was scared but finally I responded with a bit of anger myself. Why do you assume that I am not telling the truth. I'm telling you again.

I am Professor Wapello from the year 2227 and I am the inventor of a time machine. I came to this century once before and at that time, the Paz aliens controlled Earth and this ring system after they had defeated the humans in a war.

When I barely escaped at that time, I returned home and made a plan to go back to the year 2008 in order to prevent a message from being sent into space that the Paz race received and came to Earth to conquer this planet.

That's preposterous the officer shouted back. We've never been invaded by any such beings as the Paz. In fact, we've never even heard of suck alien beings. Yes I shouted back. That's because I went back in time and prevented the message from being sent on October the 22nd in the year 2008.

You should really believe me because it is absolutely true. I am here now. Am I not? You have my backpack that proves what I say is true. You just need to examine it further to prove what I am telling you is the absolute truth.

You'd better not break it I shouted back over his loud words to me. I need that backpack to get back home to my century of 2227.

If it wasn't for me, people like you would be controlled by an alien race of beings that are more powerful than anything that you could possibly imagine.

I had completely lost my temper and was tired of this obtuse military officer calling me a liar.

I've got nothing else to say to you until you examine the facts and act like you have some common sense. Get out of my face I screamed at the top of my lungs.

We'll just see about that he shouted back as he turned and walked away in an angry pace.

You'll see I screamed at him in the distance. I'm sick of being called a liar when the proof of what I told you is in the backpack that you have confiscated from me when I arrived here.

They kept me in that cell for twenty four more hours while only feeding me once on what I considered disgusting food. The food was like bland oatmeal with no seasoning and served cold with a crusty triangle of bread on the side.

During that 24 hour period, I hardly saw any humans on this lower 21 column floor.

All through the night hours lying on a cold cot, I listened as the robots steadily built metal machinery that I was unfamiliar with at the moment.

Whatever these robots were building appeared to be huge curved panels that were being shipped up to the upper Ringworld.

I surmised that they were possibly adding on to the Ringworld or maybe even completing the existing project.

Another 24 hour period passed and finally the same male security officer came to my cell and disengaged the force field and told me that I was to be escorted to the upper Ringworld to be greeted by the Federation President of Earth.

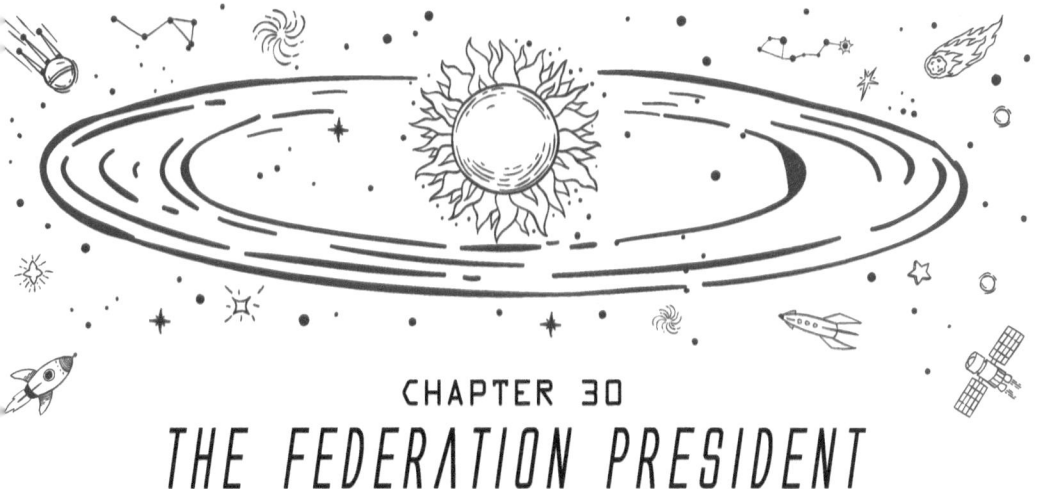

CHAPTER 30
THE FEDERATION PRESIDENT

I was first taken to a shower facility and issued military style clothing that was camouflage blue-green. After a welcomed shower,

I was then escorted by the same arrogant guard to the elevator to the upper Ringworld.

This time the guard who had viciously questioned me before had very few words to say to me as we rode the twenty minute ride to the top of Pylon 21. The elevator pivoted 180 degrees and slowed to a soft stop.

The door slid silently open to reveal a different view that I had the first time that I visited this century.

The walls and lining of the Ringworld were brilliantly colored with all of the ROYGBIV spectrum colors included.

The upper inside ceiling of the Ringworld system was clear and presented a brilliant blue Planet Earth in view. It was if you were always looking up at a pristine water world Earth on the upper floor of the inside ring.

The connecting ring spokes as far as I could see were also painted each to their own color entirely different than the golden column 21 that I had entered below at surface level. I could view the narrowing of the gold Column 21 all the way to the surface.

Shoved from behind again, I was escorted further inward around the left edge of the ring's ceiling to a large bubble shaped double guarded office that above the door had a POTEA insignia with Commander In Chief in large gold letters below.

In smaller print underneath it read,

(POTEA)(President Of The Earth Association)

There was also a statue of a rather large golden winged eagle with wings spread outward that was perched on the lookout tower high above a nuclear ocean vessel with the (POTEA) insignia also imbedded in the side of the rather large model ship .

Two other guards stood just outside the entrance and stopped us before we were allowed entrance. A few whispered words were exchanged between my guard and the other two and the door to the office was then allowed to open. The guard nudged me from behind directing me to enter the office complex doorway.

Two more guards inside stepped forward to verify the situation. I was a bit confused. Was the office of the Presidency of the World now stationed here inside the Ringworld? At present I had no detailed answers. I was scanned for hidden weapons and then allowed to enter another doorway where the head commander in chief sat starring down at a report that I assumed was about my presence here in this century.

The lady that sat behind the desk looked up at me sort of confused as to the realness of the situation.

She stood up and addressed me as Professor Wapello and introduced herself as President Carlotta Simpson of the World Federation of Planet Earth.

I immediately reached out to shake her hand but one guard interceded and explained that no one is allowed to shake the hand of the Federation President.

Sorry I explained. In my century it was common practice to greet people in such a manner. No problem President Carlotta explained. We understand the practices of the past but society had to ban hand shakes due to viruses that had troubled society for decades.

She spoke firmly. Mr Wapello, I do apologize for your early treatment but you must understand that it took us some time to verify your identity and the truth of your statements.

I immediately asked her was the president of the USA no longer allowed in this present year.

She responded that in the year 2818, a new world order had been established and all nations began electing the POTEA and now all answer to one leader. That Leader at the moment is Myself. World wide elections have been had every decade since the beginning of that new era.

We of Earth are all one country now she explained. No matter the ocean barriers between us, We are entirely one and totally united.

Now, to this important point she continued.

It took the military a while to research your identity and the exact details of your past invention of time travel and the time machine that you created in 2226.

It was discovered that in the year 2750 that the Talaxia power source that made time travel possible had began to malfunction and cause the Earth to tilt too much on its axis.

It took the cooperation of many nations to dismantle the Talaxia power source and to devise a better method to stabilize Earth's axel tilt.

In the year 2890 all nations joined together to begin building the present ring system on the equator to magnetically stabilize the unstable Earth axel tilt and rotation rate.

The Ringworld construction took over a century to build and was first completed to the point of habitation in 2992.

In fact, the many robot laborers of the lower levels are still presently building machined parts to add on to the present Ringworld's existing structure.

The Ringworld's existence also allows the surface highways to be magnetically powered so that surface vehicles can travel just above the highways in a U shaped magnetic field without friction to their precise destinations.

Installed on the underside of each of the thirty six column structures that support the Ringworld, is a Laser powered microwave projection device. Each column in a sequence projects a high powered microwave burst deep inside the molten rock under Earth's equator region.

Between the hours of eleven PM and one AM each night on the shadowed Earth side, no humans are allowed on the surface outside while the microwave projection is occurring from each specific pylon.

Once the Earth's undersurfaced shadow side is charged with microwaves, as the Earth and the Ringworld's terminator begins rotating towards the sun's light, electricity is harvested and runs up each pylon and is then combined with solar panel electricity on the outer side of the Ringworld and used to power this entire Ringworld and also all the needs of Planet Earth on the surface.

Electricity is stored and combined with solar panel power on the Ringworld's outer edge to allow the Ringworld system to have all the necessary electricity to sustain the Ringworld.

This microwave broadcast is continuous from each pylon in turn approaches the specific time period between 11 PM and 1 AM on the dark side of Earth's shadow as it rotates. Then, as the Earth rotates towards its star at the sunlit terminator, the charged surface is stripped of its electrons and transferred to the bottom of the lit side of the Ringworld to allow the electricity to be combined with solar power panels on the outside circumference of the Ringworld in order to forever supply the Ringworld with its total power needs.

Enough electricity is created to power the entire Earth's population with all the power they will ever require.

Madam President continued explaining.

Wherever you are on the night side of Earth, Between the hours of 11 PM and 1 Am, humans must not venture outside on the surface if they live within a thousand kilometers north or south of the Earth's equator.

Between those two specific night hours, if a human were to be on the surface in that area without protection, the microwave rays would cause their death within sixty seconds.

The rows of homes in the twelve hundred kilometer area are lined with microwave protection to keep humans safe while inside their homes during those two hours.

The reason that all of this is being explained in detail to You Professor Wapello, is that You Sir are a very famous individual in our present historical archives.

We have it recorded in our historical banks as to how you and your time travel device saved Earth from being invaded by the omnipotent Paz aliens by transporting in your time machine back to the year 2008.

Only You Professor Wapello have the exact memory of what it was like during those horrific days of the Paz's control of humans of this world.

However, we do know that it was you that changed Earth's past to allow the present future to become what it is in this present year of 3000.

As President of Earth's entire Federation, We of the Earth's Federation are deeply honored to meet you in person and bestow upon you this golden Federation medal of honor in extreme gratitude of what you accomplished for the betterment of Planet Earth. This golden medal bears the insignia of Forever Grateful of which we truly are.

Had it not been for your journey back in time to the year 2008, Planet Earth would now be controlled by the Paz aliens and humanity would not have a successful future.

Sir, we are indeed in your gratitude and wish to honor you in a 7 Earth rotation celebration.

But, there is a stipulation that we must inform you of before you are allowed to return back to the year 2227.

All of this years present memory and details of the Ringworld's existence will have to be wiped from your brain before you are allowed to return home to your time.

This stipulation Professor Wapello is not a request. It is a necessity and a certainty before you are allowed to return to your century.

The reason for this stipulation is, that if you had any knowledge of this present centuries progress and technology, this century and all of it's present details would not be allowed to be as it is being explained to you now.

If this stipulation of mind erase is agreeable to you, You will be allowed to explore the Ringworld for seven rotations without restriction while We of the Ringworld Federation celebrate and honor your presence here.

But, before that can be allowed, you must commit voluntarily right now to the mind erase proposition that I have just explained to you.

There is one more stipulation that I as President of Earth's Federation must explain to you before you make a decision. It is not meant as a threat but, if you decide to not commit to the mind erase, we can not allow you to return home to your time.

Yes you do have a free choice but if you do not agree to a mind erase, the Federation can not allow you to go back to your century with knowledge of this future.

If you had that knowledge, the future would not exist as it does in the year 3000. If you chose to do so, You will be allowed 24 hours to decide your fate.

I as Federation President will await your answer and act accordingly. You are under no obligation to respond until the 24 hour period has expired.

Madame President I responded. There is no need to wait 24 hours. I can give you my definite answer right now. I will commit to the mind erase now as I too understand the importance of this requirement before I am allowed to return home.

My answer is Yes, I do agree to the mind erase as long as you only erase my memories of my time here.

Very well President Carlotta Simpson replied.

You will be allowed uninhibited free access to the Ringworld's entire circumference for the next seven days and on the eighth day at 11 AM your knowledge of existence here will be erased and shortly after that time, you will be returned to your century with only the knowledge that you were here but you will not remember any details of the year 3000.

I as President of the Federation shall make the next seven Ringworld rotations a Earth Wapello holiday celebration for all future times. But, at the end of the 7 day ring rotation, You must be deprogrammed to forget everything that you have learned in your visit here in the year 3000.

You understand the reason why is because that your memory of this time could very easily change the future itself. I understand completely I replied.

Very well she stated. So be it. I will immediately make it so. Let the Wapello holiday begin.

CHAPTER 31
WAPELLO HOLIDAY

The news and details of the Wapello Holiday was spread out above and below Earth in the media across the entire planet. Everywhere you looked there was a picture of my face as I began my 7 days of exploration above and below on the earth's surface.

Many details of how the electric hybrid microwave solar pulses enabled the ring system and roadways to be powered as the rotating Earth's terminator continuously turned towards the Sun's morning light.

The panels that the robots were making were to be added to an extensions of the ring system to prepare the existing ring system in the future to become a double ring system and perhaps some day in the distant future to even become a triple ring system.

The ring system that was attached to ground level on Earth, each existed spaced approximately 700 miles apart and the 36 equal spaced columns always gave gravity to the outer floors of the ring as the planet rotated.

The ceilings facing Earth of the inside ring were clear opaque and always presented a beautiful view of the Earth and the blue Oceans below.

My journeys to the magnetic roadways below that existed to enable travel between beautiful cities all along the equator region were filled with fascinating technology explanation that mere words were very hard to explain.

Space ports existed above each pylon on the outer ring system, ferried many citizens to the Moon, Mars and other base stations in the solar system.

A Moon City that I visited was well on its way to supporting a population of a half million humans that prospered supporting by huge mining operations.

I can easily say that before my time here in this century, these seven days were the most fascinating days that I would never be allowed to remember once I was sent back to my century.

Unfortunately, there did come a time after seven wonderful celebration rotations that I was to report to the military establishment and be put through the past 7 days of mind memory erase.

That time arrived way faster than I had realized.

Here I existed upon a time when I was strapped down with my backpack attached and put to sleep to perform the procedure that would erase my memories of all that I had seen and learned while I had visited this grand peaceful year of 3000.

CHAPTER 32
UNCERTAINTY

My very last memory was a hospital procedure that put me asleep and I awoke again in my own year of 2227 with no memory of any of my time travel events or when or where I had been.

I awoke that day in my laboratory.

I remember opening my eyes from a deep sleep and asking several questions to Briana. What happened? Did the time machine malfunction? Did my trip to the past somehow change the future or even make it disappear completely?

Perhaps humans were not meant to know the future or change the past but somehow I knew that I had been to both. But, the memory of the future was always just out of reach of my thinkable grasp.

If only I could live so long as to see it for myself with my own eyes.

Except for the journey to the past, that was the only memory that I had knowledge of.

The journey to the future seemed merely a dream of thought. But the Forever Grateful medal I wore upon awakening, was a medal that I had no idea of what it represented. I was a good dream indeed.

CHAPTER 33

MY OLD AGE

I Professor Wapello am now retired from service and in the year 2265 my Lab and time machine were dismantled by the government for fear of extreme detriment to earth's future population.

Presently, at age 87, I sometimes sit out on my country front porch and scan the cloudy skies above and wonder what the future will be like.

Surely someone knows the answer. Possibly one day soon that answer will be revealed. Then again, That's what the future is. A place in the time continuum that we humans haven't reached yet.

I sometimes have flashbacks that seem just out of reach of my perception. I'm not sure anymore of any details.

With the exception of 2008, My memories of future time travel had been erased. My dreams of the events could never be erased as my rocking chair squeaks it's rhythm of provoked thought that prevails late into the darkness of this fascinating starry planet earth night sky of 2267.

All I know for sure is that this memory loss disease that I have contracted recently has taken a toll on what I once was.

I'm just content that my adventures of my youth are recorded in the archives of historical data.

Even though memories have been wiped from my personal knowledge. It was a price that I agreed to pay for the betterment of The Electric Ringworld Earth and humanities future existence.

Best Regards to All.

May you future always be as rewarding as mine was.

Forever Grateful for your Acknowledgement

Professor Irric Wapello

ABOUT THE AUTHOR

Full Name, Donald Eric Wilkins. But! I have always gone by Eric Wilkins my entire life and I always will.

Born, 1157 pm December 24, 1950

Henderson N. C.

Loved Astronomy from early age.

Lived many years on this Fantastic Spaceship Earth.

My Bucket List is almost full and I will soon go on to explore the Universe.

The Earth is moving toward Leo at the dizzying speed of 390 kilometers a second. That's a little over 242 miles per second.

You're on it too. God speed!

www.ingramcontent.com/pod-product-compliance
Lightning Source LLC
Chambersburg PA
CBHW030355180626
46812CB00007B/2886